SWARTHYFACE

Kennedy Balfour, ex-RAF in post-war Britain, helps a frightened young woman on a train, but doesn't realise what he's getting into. He only knows that Delia Thomas is beautiful, and terrified of the man following her. Apparently the man, known as 'Swarthyface', is a criminal mastermind and his main target is the girl's father. And if Balfour persists in protecting the girl and her father, then one of them would die . . . and that someone might very well be himself . . .

NORMAN LAZENBY

◆

SWARTHYFACE

Complete and Unabridged

LINFORD
Leicester

First published in Great Britain

First Linford Edition
published 2009

British Library CIP Data

Lazenby, Norman A. (Norman Austin)
    Swarthyface - - (Linford mystery library)
    1. Suspense fiction.
    2. Large type books.
    I. Title II. Series
    813.5′4–dc22

    ISBN 978–1–84782–682–4

Published by
F. A. Thorpe (Publishing)
Anstey, Leicestershire

Set by Words & Graphics Ltd.
Anstey, Leicestershire
Printed and bound in Great Britain by
T. J. International Ltd., Padstow, Cornwall

This book is printed on acid-free paper

1

A face at the window

Kennedy Balfour — late Flight-Lieutenant Balfour of the RAF — knew the girl was acting strangely. He lit a cigarette to conceal the fact that he was watching her. The train rumbled on with painful slowness, and the heat of the afternoon made him sleepy. His legs sprawled across the carriage and stuck under the opposite seat. The girl, sitting in the corner, did not seem to notice Kennedy's long feet, but she had glanced at his bulk.

He wondered if the glance was one of apprehension or appreciation. Idle thoughts flickered in his brain. Surprising that this girl and he should have the carriage all to themselves. Surprising that she should peer into the corridor almost every fifteen seconds. Surprising — or was it — that she should have written two letters with a stub of a pencil and then torn them up.

The girl was extraordinarily pretty, even though she was nervously biting her lip. She was hatless and her hair was a sort of warm brown. Now and then her blue eyes would meet his — and quickly dart away.

She was dressed very simply in a thick brown coat, and, possibly on account of the heat, the coat was open disclosing a pinstriped dress, which spoke eloquently of a first-class dressmaker. Kennedy looked at her legs. They were shapely legs and bare of any covering. Kennedy looked at the carriage ceiling again, and blew out smoke.

The girl had placed the scraps of torn paper in her handbag and she half-rose once more to look into the corridor.

This time she apparently noticed what she dreaded to see, for she withdrew sharply into the carriage and gasped audibly.

'There's something worrying you,' said Kennedy calmly. 'Whatever it is, I shouldn't worry.'

She was plainly nervous, but her brain was still cool for her to retort: 'Perhaps you have never had anything to worry about.'

'No?' said Kennedy, amusedly.

Then inconsequentially she added:

'I wish I could get off this train without being seen.'

'There are only two ways to alight from a train,' said Kennedy. 'One, you wait until it stops at a platform, and, two, you jump while the train is in motion. What have you been up to?' he asked.

He received no reply, but even with his quick reaction he was taken by surprise. The girl moved towards him quickly, sat very close to him with her face on his shoulder. She had her back to the carriage door leading to the corridor. He caught the subtle, fragrant odour of some perfume she used. Her nearness was disturbing and not only because it was unexpected.

She placed an arm round his neck. He decided she had strength in her slim arms.

'What's the idea?' he asked.

'Stay like this until he passes!' she whispered fiercely.

'Who passes?'

'You'll soon see him. He's coming down the corridor. Let him think we're a couple in love. He'll not bother to enter the carriage — at least, I hope not.'

'Who is 'he'? Your father or your fiancé?' asked Kennedy politely.

'Don't be a fool! This man is dangerous — don't you understand?'

'You have told me very little,' murmured Kennedy into her soft hair. 'But I don't mind if the story is a long one.'

'If you try to be clever, I'll kick you,' she said. 'Has he passed yet?'

'No one has passed — ah — too soon!'

Kennedy drew her closer, looked straight into her face, saw her wide, frightened eyes.

'An unusual looking bloke is peering into the carriage. I think we'll ignore him.'

For a moment he thought he'd kiss her to make the scene more realistic, but on second thoughts it occurred to him she would form a wrong judgment of him. That would never do.

Then ten seconds later he said softly:

'The bloke has gone. Is he the one you want to avoid? If so I don't blame you.'

Still she did not move.

'What was he like?' she asked.

'He had shoulders and arms like a gorilla, and a slight stoop. He had a heavy, bullet head set on a thick neck. His eyes were jet black and they glinted. He had strong, black hair growing thick down his neck and long sideboards. His skin was rough and sallow like parchment, and he had pendulous red lips.'

She stared at Kennedy.

'That is a remarkably precise description of Swarthyface. Have you seen him before?'

'I have not,' said Kennedy. 'But during the war I learnt the trick of quick assessment. Swarthyface just describes him doesn't it? Now why the devil should he frighten you?'

'Will you see if he has actually gone?' she asked.

Kennedy rose — rather reluctantly — and stuck his head into the corridor. Personally he saw no reason why he should creep round in fear and trembling.

If Swarthyface came interfering he might receive a shock.

'Not in sight,' announced Kennedy, returning to the seat.

'He is following me,' said the girl, 'and he is dangerous. I must lose him before the train reaches Dartmouth,'

'I'd like to know why you're afraid of him,' said Kennedy. 'Cigarette?'

She took one from his case gratefully. He flicked a little gold lighter into flame and they lit up.

'For instance,' remarked Kennedy, 'Swarthyface cannot be the gentleman's real name.'

After a moment's hesitation she said:

'Swarthyface is a man without a country. He claims the nationality of an obscure South American republic because no other country will recognise him or grant him repatriation. His real name is Duran Garcia.'

'What's he doing to you?' asked Kennedy bluntly,

'He's doing nothing to me — as you put it. He would like to kill my father if he could place his hands on certain facts.'

Kennedy stuck his long legs under the opposite seat, thrust his hands in his pockets and stared quizzically into her eyes.

'I'm not mad,' she said. 'Swarthyface would kill my father — or anyone else — without the slightest compunction.'

'You could tell me the whole story,' suggested Kennedy. 'And oddly enough, I believe you.'

Still she hesitated. Kennedy Balfour went on:

'Honestly after one look at Swarthyface I can believe him capable of anything. If you feel like disclosing his game, you might enliven my present dull existence and I may be able to help you. My name's Balfour — Kennedy Balfour, late of the RAF.'

'I can't tell you everything, because there are lots I don't know,' said the girl abruptly. Then she smiled. 'As a start, my name is Delia Thomas.'

Kennedy grinned.

'Nice name. What about Swarthyface, though? I say, this sounds like beauty and the beast!'

'And, Mr. Balfour, you are the rescuing knight,' retorted the girl. A sudden sparkle came to her eyes as though an idea had struck her. 'Look Kennedy, if life is dull for you I can promise to enliven it if you will get out at Dartmouth. Were you leaving the train before that station?'

'I was going to see my aunt at Exeter,' said Kennedy rapidly, 'but she won't worry when I don't turn up. Dartmouth, it is. I rather like the coast. I take it that Swarthyface will be somewhere in the background?'

'He has learnt that my father has bought a house there!' burst out the girl. 'And apparently he even knew which train I was taking. He is following me. I realize that little trick we adopted when he looked into the carriage was a waste of time. He'll see me when I leave the train. He must know I got on the train. When I get off at Dartmouth, the matter will be clinched for him if he has any doubts. My father has run away from him.'

'Run away?'

Delia placed a slender hand on his arm. By the urgency in her eyes, Kennedy knew she was about to speak more fully.

'Yes. Dad ran away from Swarthyface. We lived in London for a month, and then one day we found Swarthyface on the pavement outside the flat. It was a dark, wet night, and he simply stood beside a car at the kerb, and when we looked out the windows, he looked up. Dad was afraid. We left the flat the next morning and trained to Dartmouth. Dad bought an old house there called Carstairs. He thought that perhaps Swarthyface would be lost.'

'But you returned to London, and Swarthyface got on your trail,' prompted Kennedy.

'I suppose that happened,' she said dismally. 'I should tell you that for a month Dad worked with Swarthyface — under compulsion. Then he ran away.'

Kennedy lit another cigarette.

'If I were a detective or some other equally odd character, I should have to ask how your father could be compelled to work and what it was they worked at.'

'I wouldn't be talking to a detective at any price,' was the answer. 'And you must

9

excuse me if I'm silent about your two questions. I can only say that my father is in Swarthyface's power. Swarthyface can — oh, I can't tell you the truth.'

Delia ground her cigarette with her heel viciously.

'And, as I have said, Swarthyface would kill my father if only he could secure one vital thing. Don't ask me what that is, because that is another fact about which I can't say anything.'

Kennedy rose, stretched his long, muscular form and then had to bend to peer out of the window.

'So your father is in Swarthyface's power, can be compelled to work for him — with description of work unknown. Swarthyface is capable of murder if he can only obtain some object or fact — again description unknown. And Swarthyface is apparently following you to Dartmouth — evidently wanting to clinch the fact that your father has retreated there. And now — what?'

'Anything,' said Delia Thomas.

'Not just anything,' reproved Kennedy. 'Because I'm going to Dartmouth, too, and if Mr. Duran Garcia becomes unpleasant I shall be pleased to tap his repulsive chin.'

'I don't know,' sighed Delia, 'why I told you all this. Why should you go to Dartmouth? You might get hurt, too.'

'What — me?' said Kennedy incredulously. 'I couldn't pass this up. I'm bored to tears with life since I was demobbed. And if I may speak of my own dull private affairs, I can tell you I once had two aunts in Exeter. One died. She was quite rich and she left it all to me. The other is still alive. She is quite rich, too. But perhaps she'll leave her money to a cats' home.'

A smile crinkled Delia's lips.

'Do you really think Swarthyface could lick me in a low brawl?' asked Kennedy seriously.

She looked appreciatively at his bulk. There was lithe muscle inside the faultless suit. Kennedy Balfour was a big man — but so was Swarthyface.

'Garcia has many underlings,' she said. 'He is clever, too.'

'What was in your mind when you asked me to stop on until the train gets to

Dartmouth?' he asked.

'I wondered if you would like a job, but now you tell me you have money.'

'A job!' He smiled slightly. 'What sort of job?'

'I was thinking of a five-pound-a-week bodyguard,' said Delia squarely. 'It just occurred to me when I looked at you but — '

'I'll take it,' said Kennedy quickly, 'before the news gets around and there is a queue.'

'But — ' she began to protest.

'I'm signed on,' declared Kennedy. 'You offer and I accept.'

Under long lashes her eyes travelled downwards, watching him.

She was smiling to herself.

'It was just a sudden idea,' she repeated. 'We have to fight Swarthyface, and Dad cannot appeal to the police or anything like that.'

'You still haven't told me everything,' he reminded.

'I might — later,' she said softly.

'Well, we're getting off the train long before Dartmouth,' stated Kennedy. 'At

Taunton, to be precise.'

'For heaven's sake — why?'

'I've a pal at Taunton, and, incidentally, I'll teach Swarthyface a lesson and give him to understand I'm not on his side.'

2

On the Trail

They left the train at Taunton, and Mr. Duran Garcia, standing beside an open carriage door caught sight of Delia and Kennedy and his eyes narrowed. He drew reflectively on a long yellow cigarette, and then moved slowly across the platform in their wake.

Kennedy was lugging two cases with ease, and at the same time managed to tender his and Delia's ticket. They passed through the barrier and out into the street.

'I've simply got to reach Dartmouth today. Dad is expecting me,' said Delia for the third time.

'We'll get there,' said Kennedy cheerfully. 'So long as there are such things as taxis and buses. Is Swarthyface still tagging along?'

'I think so. At least he'll be puzzled,' admitted Delia.

14

'He'll experience a more painful emotion before long,' said Kennedy calmly.

Delia gave her companion another scrutiny. This huge man was evidently the impulsive type, and he had hustled her into a move she never intended to make. She felt rather helpless. It was a long time since she had felt that way.

'We don't want a taxi,' said Kennedy. 'We might lose Swarthyface that way. We'll stretch our legs. Swarthyface is bound to be puzzled, for he couldn't expect this.'

They traversed an old part of the town, came presently to the open countryside and took a track up a hill studded with wild raspberry canes and brambles.

'This is where we hide,' declared Kennedy. 'Behind these bushes. Down!'

'Indeed!' Delia stood doubtfully. This surprising young man expected her to obey his most idiotic orders without question. Well, she didn't intend —

Kennedy caught her hand, pulled her down behind the screen of canes.

'Your enemy might appear any moment,'

he snapped. 'I want to sock him in the eye for having the impertinence to follow you. So duck down here. Don't worry about my intentions — I've only one at the moment and that is to teach Mr. Garcia a lesson.'

Delia sat down dutifully. She looked very solemn. Sitting so intimately in this sheltered spot reminded her that this was the second time that day she had been brought into this sort of contact with Kennedy Balfour. She admitted she had no real objection to his presence — Kennedy was a *man* and very much in contrast to some of the pimply youths who had sought her company over the last three years since she left college. She caught his twinkling grey eyes, and her own dropped under long lashes.

Kennedy had noticed this charming trick. He told himself he liked it. But there was work to do. He focussed his eyes on a spot down the hill from which he expected Swarthyface to emerge.

In a matter of minutes the gorilla-like form of the man came slowly up the narrow track. Swarthyface was wearing a double-breasted suit of flamboyant chalk stripes, and this gave him the bulk of an ox. His heavy, black head moved slowly from side to side as he scrutinised the hill, looking for the persons whose actions had puzzled him.

Kennedy jumped out from behind the canes just as Swarthyface came ponderously to within five yards of their hiding place.

'Well, well! You are looking for this lady, I believe?'

The ludicrous way in which Swarthyface's thick lips parted and almost gaped caused Kennedy to grin. The other man stood and the only indication of his emotions were the dangerous glints in his jet-back eyes. Kennedy realised within a few seconds that here was a man who could be dangerous, but the childish way in which he had been ambushed made Swarthyface ridiculous.

'You are a young fool,' stated Duran Garcia. 'You are meddling with something that does not matter to you. If this is your idea of tactics, you will only make me laugh.'

He turned to go, but Kennedy snapped: 'Stay where you are!'

Swarthyface halted, turned. His heavy arms seemed to swing from his shoulders menacingly — a fact that did not escape Kennedy's notice.

'I'm issuing a warning,' said Kennedy, 'but I can see now that it will have little effect. Still, here it is: Scram, get lost, beat it! Get me? Take a walk back to garlic-land or wherever you were spawned. Leave Miss Thomas alone and forget those ideas concerning her father.'

Swarthyface made a gesture of contempt with his hands that was pure Latin.

'So you lead me what you call a silly dance to talk your foolish talk. If I meet you again it may be you will tremble with fear.'

'I can hardly imagine it,' said Kennedy, 'And I hoped you would follow us here because it is an ideally secluded spot.'

And Kennedy's hand shot out. His strong fingers closed round the other man's coat collar like a crane grab. He jerked like a deep-sea fisherman hauling in some monster from the ocean. Swarthyface uttered an exclamation in Spanish.

Kennedy had no illusions regarding his abilities. He knew, however, that he could smash a door-panel with a gloved fist; that he could lift a medium-sized man with one hand; and that he had had exactly twenty-seven fights in the roped ring while serving with the air force. Moreover, he knew a few dirty tricks, picked up from a few doubtful characters who frequented a low-type dockside gymnasium on the Thames.

All of which gave him confidence.

Obviously Swarthyface was a tough nut. The man had the physique of a mountain bear or an African gorilla.

Could he use his strength?

Kennedy discovered suddenly that the other man had undoubtedly moved in nefarious circles. Swarthyface whipped a fist immediately to Kennedy's stomach.

The usual act of a cunning ruffian who believes there is only one way to cripple his opponent.

But Kennedy's brain had covered such a possibility, and he dived for Swarthy-face's plunging fist. He caught it and jerked. Swarthyface, despite his weight, was impelled forward, and as he moved, Kennedy let go the other's fist and gave him a neat uppercut to the jaw.

The blow was strong, but not all Kennedy's weight lay behind it. Kennedy stepped back a pace; and with precise judgment rammed a right and left to the other's jaw. Swarthyface recovered, and with a snarl plunged again for Kennedy's bowels.

Kennedy knew he could beat the huge Latin — knew it the moment Swarthyface tried to repeat his first blow. In a ring he could have danced round his opponent. In the open rough and tumble, Swarthyface was obviously relying upon a few dirty tricks such as his two slaughterous blows to the stomach. Kennedy knew that had they landed he would have been a writhing, pain-wracked object, and at the mercy of the other.

But they had not landed.

Kennedy punched with grim enjoyment. *Thud! Thud! Thud!* One could enjoy punishing a man who so obviously needed chastising.

Swarthyface landed a crashing body-blow. Kennedy had expected another below the belt, but the other had changed course, swinging upwards. Kennedy took the punch with an automatic gasp, retaliated with the usual follow-up. Swarthyface grunted upon receiving the right hook. His arms widened, and, crouching, he rushed in.

He was attempting to wrestle with Kennedy. Apparently he thought he could smash his opponent to the ground by sheer weight and then despatch him with a few blows.

With such a wide target, Kennedy planted a few potential knockouts. Definitely they would have laid out any ordinary man. They definitely halted Swarthyface. He panted and made animalistic noises. Blood streamed over his chalk suit. His natty tie was a wreck.

Kennedy came right in and punched as though he were breaking down doors. The other man's arms tried to ward off, but only partly succeeded. Each blow brought a gasp, and then suddenly Swarthyface stumbled and fell.

To the gorilla-man's credit it must be stated he was on his feet as quickly as his condition would permit. Kennedy eyed him grimly.

'You can scram now or come in for more,' he said.

'You will live to regret this,' mouthed the other. 'I have made many enemies — you I will hate most. Next time I will kill you.'

'Goodbye,' said Kennedy quietly. 'And why not think over my little statement? Leave Miss Thomas and her father alone.'

Swarthyface stumbled away down the track, but Kennedy had seen the gleam of hatred in his glinting eyes.

There was blood on Kennedy's lip, and his shoulder ached. He attempted to straighten his tie, and Delia came forward.

'Let me help,' she said. 'You are hurt!'

'I deny it. Swarthyface merely scratched me.'

'I — think — I enjoyed seeing him punished,' said Delia simply. 'After all he has done to my father, I cannot feel any pity. If you only knew the mental torture Dad has undergone — ' She broke off.

They found a little stream, and with the aid of Kennedy's large handkerchief and Delia's mirror he was made presentable.

'And now we resume our journey,' said Kennedy.

'To see your pal?' suggested Delia.

'Yes. Old Clive Fordingale. Never mention the second part of his name. He hates it. Clive was my navigator in the war, and we — well it doesn't matter now.'

'You had adventures?'

'More or less. Well, if we can induce Clive to come to Dartmouth we might have a chance of smashing this Swarthy-face menace.'

'I see. So that is your idea! But I can't afford another bodyguard.'

'If Swarthyface is seriously a menace, we'll need two men. I might be away sometime — I might have to leave you and your father. Swarthyface might get at you in my absence. That's where Clive will be useful, though I warn you he has very few brains.'

Delia smiled.

'Perhaps Mr. Fordingale might have

some other engagements.'

'There you go,' groaned Kennedy. 'Never say that name in front of Clive. He would like to be known as plain Smith, but his people would object and they hold the family wealth — you understand? Clive will cancel all engagements when I tell him I have found another enemy as distinct from the war.'

'I should dearly like to learn how we will reach Dartmouth today,' said Delia.

As if he had heard the suggestion for the first time, Kennedy wrinkled his brow to consider.

'What about a bus or a taxi? But say, Clive has a huge car! Problem solved.' He grinned amiably.

'I hate to mention it, but there is another problem looming up,' returned Delia.

'What is it?'

'I am simply ravenous.'

'Solution simple!' declared Kennedy, 'We shall collect Clive and dine somewhere.'

They strolled briskly and turned down a broad thoroughfare.

Delia and Kennedy were young people and had shelved their problems for the moment, but Duran Garcia, known to his many shady associates as Swarthyface, dwelt upon his weals and indignities. He entered a public wash-and-brush-up, not without drawing a few curious looks, and made his appearance less remarkable.

Then he left and made for a telephone booth. He dialled the exchange for long distance. Eventually he was speaking through to London.

'Garcia speaking. That you, Lebb? That is good. I hoped to find you in. Listen, I want you to travel down to Dartmouth. Yes, yes. Today. I have work for you that you will like, and I think if you bring Cleavely with you it will be much better. I am speaking from Taunton. The girl is playing some fool trick, and she has found some young fool man to help her. Him I will kill some day. Perhaps you can kill him for me, Lebb.'

Swarthyface's clipped accent poured rapidly into the receiver and apparently he was regardless of his words being overheard by the exchange. He continued:

'The girl she left the train at Taunton, but I know her father is in some place at Dartmouth. The house is called Carstairs, I think. So you and Cleavely — I will meet you when you get off the ferry at Dartmouth. Perhaps not too openly, but I shall be there. We shall get what we want from Thomas, with no more delay. There has been enough delay. *Sapristi!*'

And Swarthyface left the 'phone booth with hatred for his enemies boiling inside him.

As he made inquiries about transport to Dartmouth, Delia and Kennedy blithely entered Clive Fordingale's home.

3

Meet the Relatives

The Fordingale home was a huge place on the outskirts of Taunton. Delia and Kennedy were admitted by a sedate butler, who recognised Kennedy and led him to Clive Fordingale's private study.

'You are fortunate to find Mr. Fordingale at home, sir,' murmured the butler.

Presently they were greeted by Clive. Delia saw a cheerful young man with carroty hair and a small bristly red moustache. He began to pump Kennedy's hand energetically.

'Gosh! Kennedy Balfour. It must be months since that last do at — ' He broke off, catching Kennedy's warning eye and realising some things were better left unsaid in the presence of young ladies.

'Delia — this chump is Clive you-know-the-rest. Clive — Delia Thomas, who is in need of gallant adventurers.'

'Charmed,' said Clive promptly. 'Gosh, Kennedy, what do you mean — 'adventurers'. You ought to know we had our last adventure when we left the RAF.'

'Wrong, old boy,' corrected Kennedy. 'Delia and I are about to bring old man adventure into your life again — unless the whole show is a fizzle in which case we'd better end up by having a drink.'

Clive raised carroty eyebrows, looked at Delia and Kennedy with a grin. At that moment he seemed distinctly brainless.

'Well, how do we start — this whatever-it-is?' demanded Clive.

'I have started it,' said Kennedy.

'Er — really, old boy?' Clive stared at the floor for inspiration.

'I should really like to get to Dartmouth,' said Delia.

She had been listening with compressed lips, and her words conveyed some of her annoyance.

'First a spot of lunch,' said Kennedy calmly. 'And then we can talk,'

Clive immediately suggested they should partake of lunch at the Fordingale expense.

For nearly an hour they talked over the

table and many cigarettes were smoked. Finally Clive took them round to a large garage where a huge Daimler lay. Clive had hurriedly packed a small bag and stuffed his wallet with money. He drove the car out and Delia and Kennedy climbed in.

'To Dartmouth and glorious Devon, where we engage the gentle enemy and protect the innocent,' said Kennedy.

But Clive was distinctly puzzled

'I don't quite get the hang of this,' he muttered. 'What is this blighter up to? This Swarthybloke or whatever you call him. What is the game exactly?'

'That we find out in good time,' said Kennedy quietly.

Clive drove a car as though it were a Lancaster bomber and the road was intangible air. They made terrific progress. The big car took the journey easily.

They came to ancient Dartmouth, crossed the ferry and stared about them. The jumbled, terraced streets stood calm and unruffled, while further down the bay, sounds of activities came from the small shipyards.

'Foul noise,' said Clive, frowning.

'Foul life,' said Kennedy. 'Though perhaps a spell in the hammer and chisel brigade might do you good, old man.'

Clive Fordingale shuddered.

Kennedy turned to Delia,

'Which way now?' he inquired.

'Out of the town,' was the reply. 'Take the road' — Delia indicated the road winding out of the town into the hills — 'that's where the house lies. Oh, hurry. I'm so anxious to see Dad again.'

Kennedy despite his light-heartedness, knew her anxiety was real enough, and, secondly, he was determined to help her to the full extent of his power. A game it might seem at first glance, but it was a game that could become grim and fearful.

The Daimler simply soared up the inclines, and the huddle of buildings was left behind. The road climbed and twisted, leaving the harbour below, shimmering in the bright afternoon. Then the road turned away from the sea, went inland for a mile.

'Slow down,' said Delia suddenly. 'At the bottom of this road is a narrow drive with a broken iron gate. There! See it? Go along the drive very carefully.'

Clive obeyed orders. He turned up the dilapidated drive. Mud was intermingled with the gravel. Suddenly, after passing through a veritable tunnel of leafy foliage, they came upon the house.

Carstairs was old. It was large, square and undistinguished, and seemed to be settling down to decay. Ivy climbed profusely and even covered some windows. Clive brought the car up to the main entrance.

Delia was so impatient she could hardly wait for the others. Presently they climbed the flight of steps to the door and rang a bell.

'Dad has only one servant,' said Delia. 'One is all he needs, though this house is far too big, and a great deal of it is unused. In fact, Carstairs has a history — connected with smuggling, which was rampant in these parts in the olden days. There are a few secret passages and others that are not so secret — because they're easily found. But I'll tell you more later. I wonder if Dad is ill — I have a key somewhere — perhaps it will be better if we let ourselves in.'

Delia fumbled for her key, but the door opened suddenly, disclosing a tall, cavernous-looking man.

'Oh, Dekker, how is my father?'

The cavernous man smiled, Kennedy noticed his gold tooth, his large hands and the blue tattoo marks on his wrists. Dekker had an amiable look when he smiled.

'Mr. Thomas worried a little when you departed for London, Miss. But otherwise he seems perfectly happy here,' said the man who apparently had to act as butler and jack-of-all-trades in the house.

But Delia was rushing inside. She ushered Kennedy and Clive forward. Kennedy looked for some place to deposit the bags be was carrying, and noticed the dusty condition of the hall. Everything seemed to be old and worn — the carpets were threadbare and the black oak hall seats and stands were dull and chipped. Presumably Mr. Thomas had bought the place as it stood from the previous owners.

Dekker made an effort to cope with the influx of visitors, and took their coats and bags. Delia urged the two men forward, and presently they came into a large library furnished on the old vast proportions. A small man sat at a huge battered desk and he half-rose and then sat down again upon seeing Kennedy and Clive.

'Delia — Delia — you made the journey safely? Ah, I see you did, But — who — who — '

He started nervously at Kennedy's bulk and Clive, who grinned at everyone.

Briefly Delia introduced the two young men and explained Kennedy's role of bodyguard. She touched upon seeing Swarthyface in the train, and at the mention of the Latin's name, Mr. Thomas paled.

'So he has found me again! I cannot find a retreat in this country, it seems. He will hound me until I agree to give him — what — what — he seeks. We must leave this place, Delia. It is too lonely, though I had imagined that loneliness to be an advantage.'

'Leave nothing,' said Kennedy calmly.

'But we must, young man! You do not realise what Swarthyface is like. I have been tortured by him!'

'And he will not have the opportunity again,' said Kennedy. 'I have taken a complete dislike to the man, and so the affair is personal. We shall wait until Swarthyface attacks or makes some move, then we act. Perhaps we could kill him,' said Kennedy coolly. 'Would that be of any advantage?'

Mr. Dixon Thomas drew in a deep breath.

'I would breath freely for the first time in two months if that scoundrel were dead. But you cannot kill people in this country and get away with it — that is a fact I appreciate most horribly.'

Kennedy sat down on a chair, making it creak ominously.

'I'm going to ask a question that Delia refused to answer, and I don't expect you will be more explicit,' he said. 'Why cannot you obtain police protection from Swarthyface, Mr. Thomas?'

Dixon Thomas stared bitterly at some papers before him.

'For my own safety I can only reply

precisely to my most intimate friends — and so far that has meant only my daughter. I cannot tell you, young man, why I do not seek the police, for I have merely known you a few minutes, but you are free to make your own guesses.'

Kennedy shrugged.

'And Swarthyface is after some secret which you possess — is that it, sir?'

The other nodded.

'And that secret, too, must be unknown,' continued Kennedy.

'For the moment, yes,' muttered Dixon Thomas. 'Swarthyface would kill me to possess that secret. He has tortured me, but I escaped. I have worked for him — until I realized his insatiable greed and refused him the secret he needs. Swarthyface will kill me the moment he finds the secret to which I allude, but he will not kill me before that because then he would have lost the secret forever.'

'Baffling, absolutely baffling,' observed Clive unconcernedly, and he received frowns all round,

'I'll see if Dekker can concoct tea,' said Delia, and she departed more light-heartedly than she had felt for many months. Her beloved father was unharmed and there were two young men who apparently enjoyed the prospect of fighting evil men.

'I cannot easily imagine how Swarthy-face discovered I had bought this house,' said Dixon Thomas. 'It is rather remote and a long way from London.'

'When you worked for Swarthyface, where did you live, sir?' asked Kennedy.

After some hesitation Thomas answered:

'I find answering these questions brings up bitter memories. You might as well know, young man, that the work we were doing was illegal. Yes, I mean criminal activities. Swarthyface had an establishment in the heart of Liverpool. I worked there, and Delia lived there.' Dixon Thomas stared with watery blue eyes at Kennedy, apparently struck by some thought. 'And now, young man, if you are a detective and have merely gained my daughter's confidence to gain information, you have something to think about.'

'But not much,' said Kennedy dryly. 'Anyway, I'm not a detective. Such identification papers as I carry round, you can read. And I don't think Clive will have anything to hide. We want to help you, sir.'

'But I can't understand — why — ' Dixon Thomas swallowed.

'Because it's a lark,' said Clive cheerfully.

Dixon Thomas sighed. Evidently he did not think so.

Kennedy looked round the library. There were simply thousands of books, and they looked distinctly dusty.

'I suppose you bought this place lock, stock and barrel,' he murmured.

'Yes. The owner sold out cheaply. It seemed such a splendid place to hide from Swarthyface.' And Delia's father sighed again.

'And Dekker?' Kennedy murmured idly. 'Is he newly acquired?'

'No. He kept house for us when we were in London. An old friend — a very old friend — recommended him to me. He had letters from this friend.'

Kennedy nodded, and then glanced questioningly at Clive. It seemed to him that Delia had been gone a fairly lengthy time — but then tea-making without much help was a lengthy business.

A quarter of an hour passed, and Kennedy was faintly puzzled. Delia had not appeared. He got up, went to the library door and stood listening. Eventually he opened the door and walked into the passage, stared in the direction of the kitchen.

He popped his head back into the library.

'I'm going to the kitchen. Maybe Delia could do with help.' He hoped his voice sounded casual. It should be casual. Perhaps he had the jitters.

He walked swiftly to the kitchen, pushed open the door. There was no one to be seen, and a kettle steamed merrily on a modern gas stove.

Kennedy called 'Delia' several times, and walked into an adjoining room. Neither the girl nor Dekker were to be seen, and there was no sound. A feeling of foreboding smote him and he ran to several rooms all of which were deserted, and still no sign of Delia. He tore back to the library. He went over to Clive.

'Let's quit playing,' he whispered. 'Delia's been kidnapped!'

4

Persistent Enemy

Delia Thomas had found Dekker in the kitchen with an apron round his middle and numerous cupboard doors hanging open. Dekker smiled, showing his gold tooth. Delia had noticed the ornament before and had taken an unreasonable dislike to the thing, but at the moment she was feeling happier than she had felt for months and Dekker's affectation was a mere trifle.

'I'll help you, Dekker,' she said.

'Thank you, Miss Thomas.'

They were busy for some minutes and then Dekker slipped out of the kitchen,

Delia began to slice through a loaf and tried to estimate the number of slices required.

'I imagine those two men have enormous appetites — now a salad and new bread — must provide for outsize

39

appetites — and salad cream — '

A man crept softly into the kitchen. He was tall and moved with the noiseless tread of a cat. He wore an old felt hat pulled over his eyes, and covering his mouth and chin was a black scarf.

He crept forward without hesitation. His arms widened, and then he leaped the last two yards. A large hand clamped over Delia's mouth, and another arm circled her, gripping her arms to her side.

The man began to drag the girl out of the kitchen. Delia struggled after the initial shock had passed, but she was like a child in an adult's grasp. The man was strong enough to handle a horse. He dragged her over to the door leading out of the house.

Delia received only a confused impression in the next few ghastly minutes. She was gasping for breath and attempting to scream at the same time. She wriggled desperately, tried to wrench one of her arms free. She gave her attacker a run for his money but it was hopeless.

Before she had time to realise the value of locating her bearings she was dragged into some dark place. It might have been a shed or a cellar, but she could not know. Her attacker dragged her none too gently. She could hear his heavy breathing. She tried to bite his hand, but the man had skin like leather.

The place seemingly was not a cellar, for the man continued to haul her along like a sack of coals, and the darkness lay over everything. Even though her eyes should have become accustomed to the gloom, she could still see nothing but blackness. And even this blackness was streaked with red forks of light before her eyes as she struggled with beating heart and choked breath.

Then it dawned on her mind.

She was being taken down some tunnel. Her attacker was not moving in some confined space, but progressing forward all the time. If this was a tunnel, then it could only be one of the many secret tunnels and passages under the old house — passages that had been built for scores of years and almost forgotten in the passage of time.

Delia knew there were tunnels running

down to the sea, though few outlets on the coast had been found. Years of decay had choked the mouths of these tunnels.

Her legs were bruised several times as she was dragged over uneven ground, and she cried out with pain. Her attacker took not the slightest notice.

She was dragged and hauled for what seemed an age, though desperately trying to retain her wits; she estimated the time to be little over fifteen minutes.

It was horrible. If she was under Carstairs, she could be hidden from the world in fifteen minutes.

And then her captor loosened his grip. and grunted. He set her down on the rough, rocky ground. Delia subsided, because her legs felt weak and there was obviously no sense in running away in a pitch-black tunnel. She could not see her captor. If he had removed his disguise, it mattered little.

Who was he?

Undoubtedly one of Swarthyface's underlings. The man was not Swarthyface — unless Garcia had been able to alter his physical shape. Her attacker was just

42

as tall as Swarthyface, but the Latin was bulkier.

Why had she been kidnapped like this?

There could be one or two answers, but they all amounted to the same thing. Swarthyface would be able to get at her father by holding her as hostage.

Undoubtedly Swarthyface had acted speedily. In fact, it seemed incredible that she should be attacked in Carstairs when they had left Swarthyface in Taunton only a few hours ago.

Delia's captor was busy. He was making a curious metallic jangling noise. Delia listened, trying to stifle her own heavy breathing. What was the man doing?

She soon realised the metallic noise was the rasp of a key in a lock. There was the familiar scraping sound, and then the man thudded upon some object with his fist. This could only be a door, and the man was experiencing difficulty because the lock was rusted. Then came the snap of a catch jerking back.

The man swung open the door that gave stiff, creaking noises. Then his arms came towards Delia in the blackness, grasped her and began to propel her towards the door. She struggled.

Her brain grappled with the situation. She was being placed in some sort of cell. Evidently a dark hole with a door and lock from which she could not move.

'You can't do this . . . you swine . . . you . . . let me go . . . '

Delia struggled like a tigress. This might be her last chance to escape — and she might never see daylight again. Once the door clanged — Delia's imagination, whipped nearly to hysteria by the darkness and the sudden events, conjured up hideous thoughts of confinement until madness overcame her.

But her fight for freedom was futile against the other's superior strength. The man, beginning to snarl as if his patience was exhausted, almost threw her into the space beyond the door. Delia fell, tried to spring to her feet. As she scrambled forward, sobbing, she heard a stiff, rusty creak and then — *clang*!

She threw herself against the door. She discovered she was clawing at a rusted metal door, studded with numerous rivet heads. There was no projecting handle or anything that would afford a means of tugging the door open.

She fancied she heard the man's footsteps fading away, and realising her awful situation she sank weakly to the ground. She was alone in the bowels of the earth with blackness pressing all around her. No one would find her. Even if she screamed, the sound would not travel far. The dead tunnel would absorb her screams as a tomb absorbs the dead.

But Delia's feelings were only momentary weakness. She sprang to her feet, began to explore her surroundings. The door was definitely immovable. The man must have locked it, and the hinges were set into the rock and as strong as the day some ancient craftsman built them. Delia's hands began to feel the walls round her. The rock was damp and cold. She shuddered involuntarily. Nevertheless, she continued desperately with her examination. She was hoping against hope that she could discover something that her jailor had overlooked. It was, on the face of it, a forlorn hope.

The rocky cave went back a good many yards and then curved in a cul-de-sac. Delia continued to feel her way round. Nothing but cold damp rock, and then —

Her hands stopped. She had found something that was not part of the rocky wall. She slowly let her hands touch the hard object ... her fingers travelled down, touched bony ribs.

Delia backed blindly and screamed. She ran away from the ghastly fright she had received. She ran and running fell near to the iron door. Her screams choked into a sob. She steadied herself and made a strong effort to control her nerves.

For it was all nerves. Over in the corner was a skeleton — probably an age-old skeleton. It could not harm her, frightful companion though it was.

Delia sat near to the door. The door seemed to be the symbol of freedom. If only she could pass through!

She began to collect her thoughts — tried to think of cheerful things. For instance, Kennedy and Clive would soon miss her. They were not fools and would start an immediate search. Surely they would think of the old tunnels?

Uneasily Delia knew there were miles of tunnels and near the coast they emptied into natural caves. There were old stories of how in the ancient days people had gone into the caves and never appeared again.

Still there was a chance.

She hugged the door, and found a small square opening like a grill. Air came through, Vaguely she thought she detected the odour of the sea.

She began to shout. She shouted carefully and methodically, counting twenty between every shout. It seemed the only way to keep calm.

But a long time passed and there was no response.

★　★　★

Kennedy Balfour and Clive were two disconsolate and grim young men. They had roamed the house from top to bottom, found Dekker locked in an outhouse. But there was no sign of Delia,

'Get the police,' suggested Clive.

Kennedy rounded upon him.

'Use your brain, chump. The police are taboo. Delia's not in this house. Come on, we've got to organise a party to search for these damned secret passages. Mr. Thomas will have to help, and Dekker, too. They know the place better than we do. If only there was some sort of clue, but she's simply vanished.'

'In a yarn I once read,' began Clive thoughtfully, 'the girl got stolen and she dropped clues all over the place. You know — gloves, handkerchiefs, matchsticks and the like. Damned clever, I thought. Ow! Wharrer doing?'

'Kicking you!'

They came to Dekker and Dixon Thomas. The manservant was doing his best to soothe Delia's father.

'This is Swarthyface's work,' said Kennedy grimly. 'But I'm certain Swarthyface is not in Dartmouth yet. We left him in Taunton, and travelled by fast car. We did waste an hour, but if Swarthyface was able to proceed on his journey without losing some time, then he was very lucky.'

'You know, I can't understand how it is you didn't see this intruder, Dekker,' observer Clive.

'I went out, sir, as I have informed Mr. Balfour, to bring in some coal for the fires. I had noticed they were getting very low, sir. Everything happened in a most sudden and alarming manner. I was rushed into the outhouse, and the door locked. Fortunately the outhouse is quite large and so I was able to avoid soiling myself.'

Clive seemed anxious to show Dekker he believed every word.

'Oh, yes, I see. Damned convenient for the kidnapper, what? And the lock on the outhouse — one of those damned convenient things. Click! — and you are locked in. Could have locked yourself in, s'matter o' fact.'

Dekker said tonelessly: 'Perhaps, sir. But I repeat I was locked in, sir.'

Kennedy's eyes flickered over the tall manservant. Clive went on babbling unconcernedly. Dixon Thomas nervously fumbled with his fingers.

'Do you like your job with Mr. Thomas, Dekker?' questioned Kennedy. 'Doesn't this affair worry you?'

'The position is quite suitable,' said Dekker gravely. 'And I am most concerned about Miss Thomas. I am of the opinion that the police should be informed, sir.'

Kennedy turned away. There was no laughter in his face.

'Get some candles and matches and an electric torch, if there is one in the house,' he said to the manservant. 'We simply must get started on a search of these smugglers' tunnels, and you must come, too, Mr. Thomas. We can't leave you for Swarthyface.'

Dixon Thomas stood up, wiped perspiration from his brow.

'Swarthyface has beaten me,' he whispered. 'I can't leave Delia in his hands.'

Kennedy stared. Dekker was halfway across the room, and he turned, stared.

'We don't intend to leave Delia in Garcia's hands,' rapped Kennedy.

'He can have my secret,' said Dixon

50

Thomas in a low voice.

'Don't say another word!' snapped Kennedy. 'Dekker, will you get the gear I mentioned?'

Dekker left the room calmly. He collected candles, matches, ropes, and an electric torch from his kitchen. Going to a drawer, he drew out a heavy object and placed it inside his jacket pocket.

The object was an automatic revolver.

5

The Death Chamber

Jonathan Lebb was a young and callous man. His thin, peaked face disclosed these facts to the world. His black, sombre eyes were as cold as a snake's. His fingers, yellowed with incessant smoking, curled round the butt end of a small, but efficient, automatic of continental origin. Jonathan Lebb liked the feel of the weapon.

His companion, Sid Cleavely, had all Lebb's traits, though in appearance he was taller and he favoured suavity instead of lean hardness. In addition he had a licentious interest in women, and boasted of it.

They were looking for Duran Garcia, their employer.

The ferryboat already on its way back to the small village on the other side of the harbour, and Swarthyface had not made an appearance.

'I wonder if Swarthyface is actually here,' growled Cleavely.

'Quit moaning about it,' said Lebb dispassionately. When he spoke his lips barely moved. 'He's the boss, and he pays well. He'll be here. There's a job to do.'

Cleavely laughed, though his attitude of independence was false as his jewelled finger. He had debts in London, mostly because he gambled and women at any time were expensive.

'Let's quit worrying, Lebb,' said Cleavely decisively. 'We're thinking of the money. That's what I'm working for — money. And I don't trust Swarthyface no more than you.'

'Here he is,' said Lebb thinly.

They had walked a little way into the town, past the marine gardens. Swarthy-face, his chalk suit miraculously cleaned — he had walked into a tailor's shop in Taunton and paid good money to be made presentable — came swinging towards them. He walked jauntily, his heavy arms moving pendulum-like from his gorilla body.

His sallow face crinkled into an expansive smile when he noticed his lieutenants. He came abreast, turned and they walked away. Suspicious men by nature and habit, they did not intend to display their meeting to the idle gaze of the loungers near the ferry head

'I've been here an hour,' said Swarthyface. 'Got a place for the night and plenty of nights if needed — and room for you two birds.'

'Hope it's a long way from the police-station,' said Lebb in his expressionless voice.

'A little inn — and the keeper is a man after our own hearts, though I suspect he is a little timid with quiet living. Once he was fairly clever, though not clever enough to keep out of prison. I know him. I knew he lived here.'

'Clever,' commented Cleavely and in contrast to his previous words his voice was distinctly humbugging. 'How did you get here?'

'Taxi, and the driver was the son of a highway rogue,' growled Swarthyface. 'He charged me a scandalous price, and I

54

could easily have broken his thin neck like that!' Swarthyface made an expressive gesture.

'What do you want us to do?' asked Lebb abruptly.

'You know my plans regarding Dixon Thomas.'

'Some of them,' said Cleavely. 'We gave a hand with him once before.'

'You know sufficient for you to carry out orders,' said Swarthyface harshly. 'So! I want you to be — what is it? — on hand. Yes you will be on hand because although I have the fool's daughter, he may be difficult. He has surrounded himself with two stupid young men. You may have to deal with those men.'

'You've got the girl?' Lebb made it a question. He displayed no surprise.

Cleavely leered.

'Lead me to her,' he said 'Whatever you want, I'll get it.'

'How did you work it?' said Lebb carefully.

Swarthyface blew out smoke and replaced his yellow cigarette between thick red lips that pouted with satisfaction.

'You are not the only men who work for me,' he boasted. 'The girl was secured even before I arrived here. I gave orders, and my orders are obeyed. So.'

He had a pretty conceit. Lebb, watching him narrowly, knew even the conceit was dangerous.

'Where is the girl?' asked Lebb.

'Where she is safe — for the moment. If Thomas is stubborn she may have to be removed. But if he admits defeat, and I get the secret I want, then she will be found.'

'What will happen?' drawled Cleavely.

'Thomas will give in immediately, and you, my friend, will take him a message now.'

'It's all the same to me,' drawled Cleavely.

Amusement glinted in Swarthyface's jet eyes.

'Come first to The Strong Arm. That is the strange name of the inn. Then you will know where to return after delivering Thomas a message.'

'What is the message?'

'Simply that I want the pretty picture.

Dixon Thomas will know exactly what I mean. He has to deliver it to me at The Strong Arm. You, my friend, have not to see it.' Swarthyface spoke very softly. 'Remember that. I should have to punish you if you attempt to pry into what does not concern you. Also, give Thomas the usual warning that life will be full of sighs and regrets if he tries to approach the police. That, of course, he will not do.'

'These blokes with him — will they influence Thomas?' asked Cleavely.

Swarthyface scowled.

'One of them I should like to kill. Perhaps I will if our paths cross. But Thomas knows the utter futility of speaking to the police and these young men will not make him change his mind. For Thomas, like us my friends, the police are enemies.'

The Strong Arm lay among a huddle of old cottages halfway up a steep narrow, cobbled lane. Swarthyface and Cleavey had to bow their heads to enter the main door. Lebb, more stockily built, was unaffected. They found themselves in a small bar that was deserted because it was not yet opening time. Stuffed exhibits, tankards and bottles lined the walls. A faint odour of cheese and beer hung about the place. Swarthyface led them across the sawdust covered floor towards a narrow, twisting staircase. They climbed to the next floor and entered a large room in which were three beds. A huge mullioned window allowed the evening sun to shaft into the room. Dead silence hung over the inn.

'Here we shall stay. We are harmless tourists, and I do not think Dixon Thomas will be eager to accuse us of anything else.' Swarthyface chuckled huskily. 'Cleavely, you know what to do and say. Do not make a mistake.'

Cleavely nodded coolly, though he fancied there was an implied threat in the last five words.

He left The Strong Arm, went down the cobbled road. One or two locals stared at him, but it was mere curiosity. Actually Cleavely with his well-cut suit and assured air was like the usual visitor.

Swarthyface had given him complete directions so that he lost no time in finding Carstairs. The actual walk occupied some twenty minutes, and then he found himself approaching the old square house.

It was just luck that he ran immediately into a party of men crossing the weed-covered lawn. Cleavely knew Dixon Thomas at once, though the two young men were strangers to him. Cleavely eyed the bulk of the man who halted the party. Such big men were rareities, especially so when the specimen obviously carried not an ounce of superfluous fat. The other young man sported a gingery moustache. Cleavely made the mistake of assessing him as unimportant.

'Hi, you! What do you want?' Kennedy Balfour was feeling grim and indisposed to be polite.

Cleavely smiled suavely.

'Message for Mr. Thomas. From his er — friend, Duran Garcia.'

Dixon Thomas paled.

'Yes?' he said.

'Swarthyface wants the pretty picture,' said Cleavely blandly.

Dixon Thomas looked appealingly to

Kennedy. That young man strolled up to Cleavely, and at the grim light in his eyes Cleavely felt a sudden slip of his self-confidence. At close quarters Kennedy Balfour positively loomed over the other man, and Cleavely tall enough in all truth, did not like the feeling.

'What do you think has happened to Delia Thomas?' asked Kennedy.

Cleavely smiled twistedly. After all he could handle this mountainous fool.

'Swarthyface has got her. So hurry, please. I want to know if Thomas will deliver the pretty picture to an inn called The Strong Arm.'

'Yes, Thomas will deliver a pretty picture to The Strong Arm,' said Kennedy readily.

'Good,' said Cleavely. 'I thought you'd see sense. The boss is a tough customer to cross. Bring the pretty picture to The Strong Arm at nine tonight sharp. I don't suppose it matters who brings the damned thing.'

'What is the pretty picture?' asked Kennedy curiously.

Cleavely leered.

'As a matter of fact, I don't damned well know. It doesn't make much sense. I guess only Swarthyface and Thomas know — and Delia Thomas,' added Cleavely, 'Don't you know what it means, pal?'

'I don't,' said Kennedy briefly. 'That's why I asked you.'

Cleavely waved a hand nonchalantly.

'Guess I'll be going. So you're bringing a pretty picture to The Strong Arm tonight at nine?'

'I won't bring it,' said Kennedy grimly. 'But a pretty picture will crawl into the Strong Arm and long before nine. Take that, you third-rate swine!'

And Kennedy's fist smashed into Cleavely's face. Pain filled the racketeer's nerves, and blood spurted. Cleavely was completely unable to retaliate. The blow staggered him and another, much more forceful, felled him to the ground. He lay without stirring. Kennedy had knocked him clean out.

'Give me a hand to drag him in,' said Kennedy. 'We'll add him to the collection of ungodly freaks.'

Clive was willing. He grasped Cleavely's feet and Kennedy took the man's head. Swarthyface's emissary was carried feet first into Carstairs.

They took him to a deserted room. Actually the room was deserted of furniture, but in a corner a man lay bound.

The man was Dekker.

'Put this bloke beside his pal,' said Kennedy. 'We'll need a bit of rope eventually.'

'Rather a distant eventuality,' said Clive.

Dekker watched the proceedings with silent, brooding hate.

Kennedy turned to Dekker.

'Another underling of Swarthyface. Do you know him?'

'No.'

'Lucid, anyway,' observed Clive.

Dekker simply glowered, eyed the unconscious man curiously.

'What did he come here for?' he said.

'He came for a pretty picture,' said Kennedy. 'Know anything about a pretty picture?'

Dixon Thomas began to protest.

'I must ask you not to put such questions. Anyway, I doubt if Dekker knows much. Later, young man, I'll probably inform you about pretty pictures and oh, everything!'

'I don't know what you are talking about,' said Dekker.

Kennedy thought he meant it.

'Well you were clever enough, Dekker. But those tattoo marks are rather a giveaway, don't you think? I know the outline of a prison warder when I see one. Then I felt the gun in your pocket. Even so, you could have explained all that away if you hadn't turned on us. Unluckily for you I once was trained in the best way to turn a gun.'

'And you did lock yourself in that outhouse, you damned fraud,' accused Clive.

Dekker tried to spit at them.

'Swarthyface will get you. And you will never find the girl.'

'Swarthyface evidently planted you on Mr. Thomas,' mused Kennedy. 'Forged papers are easy enough to obtain. You lay low, giving full service. You were ready to act just when Swarthyface needed you most.'

'My poor girl — Mr. Balfour, we must find her — Swarthyface must have her!' Dixon Thomas had another bad attack of nerves.

'Dekker will tell us where he took her,' said Kennedy, and the ominous tone of his voice struck a chill to the bound man.

'You can all go to hell!' sneered Dekker.

'You, my friend, will be despatched there,' said Kennedy softly. 'But your pals down under won't recognise you. That would be a pity. You don't want to arrive in Hades looking like the wreck of the Hesperus, do you?'

'What the devil do you mean?' Dekker snarled, showing his gold tooth.

'Unless you spill the truth quickly,' said Kennedy in a voice that stabbed like a sabre, 'you'll find I'm worse than an atomic bomb.'

'You wouldn't dare!' Dekker spat the words contemptuously.

Kennedy saw the other was a man who could only be convinced by force and action. Kennedy came close to his man. His two fists were knotted grimly. There was one thing he was determined upon, and that was Delia's earliest recovery.

Kennedy rammed his fist into Dekker's face. Dekker's head jerked back under the impact, while his features writhed with anguish. He made an animal noise and tried to shake away his dazedness. His eyes blazed hatred.

Kennedy bent down, spent three minutes loosening Dekker's bonds.

'Now get up. I'll give you a chance to hit back. Fight, you swine!'

Clive grinned and cleared Dixon Thomas back to a corner of the deserted room. Cleavely still lay in a heap in another corner.

Dekker, burning with rage and not without crude courage, rushed at Kennedy. He was met by a murderous blow that almost dropped him. Kennedy had hit harder than he intended. He told himself he would have to pull his punches. He wanted to hurt Dekker, force the man to confess what he had done with Delia Thomas. The last thing he wanted was to knock out Dekker.

He played with the tall cavernous man. After Dekker's initial rush, his rage had evaporated to desperation. All Dekker desired was a way of escape from this huge man who was steadily beating him to pulp. Kennedy hit him scientifically where the man would feel it most. Dekker began to sob. His efforts to retaliate became almost nil. Kennedy kept on, not because he enjoyed inflicting torture, but because he could not rid himself of a picture of a girl bound or locked in some God-knows-what sort of hole.

He was determined to make Dekker speak.

After ten minutes Kennedy was beginning to feel disgusted with himself. Dekker merely circled, attempting to elude his punisher, his face a red mass and blood covering his clothes. He was groaning but still he did not speak. Clive had lost his grin. His face was expressionless. Dixon Thomas was plainly aghast.

And then suddenly Dekker shrieked.

'Leave me alone, you devil! Leave me alone. I'll tell you. The girl is in the tunnel!'

Kennedy held him up with one hand, said grimly:

'What part of the tunnel?'

Dekker panted for breath and said:

'The entrance is in the stable. The third stall — a centre slab — the passage goes right under the house — Swarthyface told me to get — hide her — until further notice.'

'I suppose he 'phoned you,' said Kennedy. 'Well, get moving, and God help you if you try to trick me. Show us where the girl is. Don't waste another minute.'

'What about this specimen?' asked Clive, indicating Cleavely.

'Let him lie. He'll come round shortly, and stagger back to his employer. Didn't I say a pretty picture would be delivered before nine?'

The three men left the house, went round to an old building that once had served as a stable. The building lay near to the rear doors of the house. Dekker went in first, followed by Kennedy.

The stone slab was not difficult to find. It pivoted without a great deal of trouble, disclosing a dark flight of wide steps. So wide were these steps leading down into a dark shaft, that Kennedy could take three short strides before reaching the next step. He had the electric torch, and he switched on, illuminating the black, wet walls of the tunnel. Kennedy paused to ascertain that, so far, they were moving in a seaward direction. Evidently this passage, built for some obscure purpose in the ancient past, led to the sea.

Dekker was seemingly defeated. He moved on, with Kennedy's torch behind him. Kennedy estimated a mile had passed, though perhaps that was a generous estimate, yet fifteen minutes had gone and they had not slackened their pace.

Then Dekker slowed. The ground was jagged and the roof uneven. The tunnel seemed to be joining a natural cave. Finally Dekker stopped at an iron door.

'She's here,' he said sullenly, and he brought out a huge iron key.

Kennedy eyed the door. Hundreds of years ago some rogues had set this barrier in place for some dark purpose.

'Open up,' ordered Kennedy.

Dixon Thomas raised his voice, shouted: 'Delia! Delia!'

There was no answer.

'Hurry with that key!' Kennedy ground out.

'She may have fainted,' said Clive Fordingale soothingly.

Dixon Thomas was terribly agitated, and Kennedy Balfour felt a little nerve twitching in his temple. If Delia were harmed . . .

Dekker fumbled, and seemed to be oddly slow. Then:

'The door is open,' he said in sullen surprise. 'The lock is turned.'

Kennedy pushed with his foot. The door went backwards stiffly, creaking dolefully. He lunged inside.

His torch flashed round the rocky cavern, shone on the dull bones of the skeleton. Kennedy exclaimed 'Damn!' and stamped right round the place. It was a damp, cold empty dungeon that had never seen the light of day.

Delia Thomas was not here. Kennedy plunged back to the door. He gripped Dekker. 'Where is she? What is the trick?'

'I left her here,' said Dekker hoarsely. 'I left her here!'

6

Strange Friend

Sid Cleavely stirred and as the mists cleared from his brain; he was able to sit up. He spent five minutes shaking his head like a dog and feeling his jaw, which seemed to be swelling painfully.

Then he remembered everything.

'The swine!' he raged. 'Swarthyface will kill the hulking swine!'

Then it occurred to him that Swarthyface would hardly be pleased at the way he had handled the negotiations concerning the 'pretty picture'. The big young man had not reacted according to plan.

'Well, Swarthyface has the girl,' muttered Cleavely. 'If they think they can cross the boss, they can think again.'

He stood up. He was surprised that he was free to move. He looked round the deserted room, went to the door and looked into the passage. He began to make his way down the thinly carpeted passage, smoothing his black oily hair as he walked. It soon became apparent that the house was empty. He did not meet anyone as he cautiously looked into various rooms. Some of the rooms were not furnished, and others were studded with dustcovers draping settees and the like.

Cleavely did not want to meet the big young man again. It had occurred to him to scram — to get back to his employer with the astonishing news that the other camp had rebelled. But seeing an apparently empty house was too much for his curiosity.

Cleavely did not know Dekker, or that the man was an underling of Duran Garcia's.

Cleavely did not know where the girl had been taken — he did not really care.

He was thinking of leaving while the going was good, when the words 'pretty picture' came into his brain.

'I wonder what the hell it means?' he muttered. 'Can't be a damned picture the boss is after.'

He peered carefully into a room that was obviously a library, and used at that. A desk stood near to a fireplace, but the fire was cold. Cleavely went over, saw the telephone immediately and was struck by a sudden idea.

He could not understand why the occupants of the house had gone out, leaving him to get away. But they had, and, characteristically, he stopped thinking about it.

Here was a 'phone — and he had taken the trouble to note the 'phone number of The Strong Arm before he left!

He dialled rapidly, while his eyes flickered nervously to the door and back. The sun was setting and dusk was shading the room. Cleavely did not want to be caught napping. Soon he was speaking to Duran Garcia.

'The big feller knocked me down . . . wouldn't listen . . . though I did tell him and Thomas your message . . . I guess they're worried about the girl . . . they're out the house now . . . that's how I'm 'phoning . . . maybe they're looking for the dame . . . '

Cleavely heard Swarthyface hiss into the receiver at the other end. Swarthyface spoke angrily.

'He is a bigger fool than I imagined . . . and he must have Thomas completely influenced . . . I shall warn Thomas for the last time . . . then the girl . . . she will suffer . . . '

'What about the pretty picture?' asked Cleavely eagerly. 'If it's in the house, maybe I could get it. Tell me what to look for. Thomas's desk is right in front of me. Will it be there?'

But Swarthyface's voice came back to him full of menace.

'Forget your fool idea. The pretty picture will not be found so easily, and it is not for you to see. Come back here — no — I think I have an idea that is good. Yes — hide somewhere in the grounds of the house. Lebb and I are coming over by car. We shall hire a taxi, if we can find one in this fool town. Have you not seen Thomas' manservant?'

'I saw no one but the two strangers and Thomas.'

'Then Dekker must be playing his part,

helping to search for the girl.' Swarthy-face chuckled. 'If you see the manservant Dekker, try to contact him, tell him we're coming over to raid Carstairs. We will make one good attempt to get the pretty picture.'

'Who is Dekker?' asked Cleavely.

'Dekker is the manservant in my employ, you fool. He is the one who got the girl.'

And Swarthyface rung off abruptly. It was as well for the unscrupulous Latin that no one at the exchange listened intelligently to the conversation. Metallic voices meant nothing to tired operators.

Cleavely sidled out of Carstairs. In one sense he was glad to escape. His jaw felt badly bruised, and he didn't want its condition to be worsened. He was distinctly jumpy at the thought of meeting Kennedy Balfour again.

He went slinking into the thick clumps of trees and bushes, making his way down to the broken iron gate. He intended to wait here for Swarthyface and Lebb. He had not seen Dekker, and did not feel too enthusiastic about conducting a search.

The next time he set off to contact Thomas and his violent associates, he would pack a gun and let the big fellow have it. That was supposing there was another time.

Sid Cleavely fell to thinking about the pretty picture. The two words sounded damned silly to him, but there could be no doubt that Swarthyface was deadly serious about a 'pretty picture'. What the blazes was he after?

Cleavely knew there must be money somewhere — and big money. More than the few miserable pounds that Swarthyface would hand out to his underlings . . . must be thousands in it . . . Dixon Thomas had a secret and a valuable one . . .

Lebb knew something. Lebb had worked in Liverpool for Garcia, unlike Cleavely.

What the hell sort of work had Lebb done in Liverpool? Cleavely made a mental note that he would endeavour to pump his colleague.

Cleavely fell to thinking about his debts and his women in London. He hated his creditors, but liked his women. If he could only get hold of some real money, his problems would be solved.

If he could only persuade Lebb to work hand in hand against Swarthyface . . .

The thought was a startling one, though it was not new. Always in the back recesses of Sid Cleavely's mind there dwelt plans to double cross his partners, whoever they might be at the time.

Double crossing Swarthyface would be dangerous — extremely dangerous. Could it be done? Cleavely stood and thought about it.

He had an appreciable time in which to think.

It was while he stood in the shelter of the thick bushes he saw a man and a girl come slowly towards the broken iron that gave entrance to the drive. The girl was wearing a pinstripe dress that was entirely spoilt by slime and mud. On her pale face were streaks of dirt. Cleavely hid himself completely and watched.

The man was old and a peculiar character. He was bent, and he trailed along beside the girl as though averse to approaching too close. His scanty locks were covered by a hideously greasy fisherman's cap, and his ragged trousers were equally filthy. His hands, black as the earth, hung sloppily by his side. His cheeks were white with bristly whiskers. He was muttering indistinctly to himself and glancing fearfully at the girl with every yard.

He seemed reluctant to follow the girl, and she had to beckon him frequently.

Cleavely watched them with a frown. Who were they? The girl was making for Carstairs.

An extraordinary suspicion attached itself to Cleavely's mind. Could this be Thomas' daughter? It was perhaps a wild idea, for Swarthyface had the girl in safe keeping. Yet . . .

Why was this girl making for Carstairs with such obvious familiarity? And why was she in such a dirty state?

Cleavely could not find answers to his questions, and the girl and old man passed up the muddy drive. Cleavely was left frowning.

While his mind played with a variety of

incredible ideas, time passed. Presently he heard the sound of a car braking a little way down the road. Another minute and two men approached with heavy, wary footsteps.

'Here is a gun, my friend,' said Swarthyface. He halted with Lebb in the shadow of the bush. The night was rapidly darkening, and a quiet was descending over the countryside. Somehow it seemed a silence full of menace to Cleavely. He started to explain his failure, but Swarthyface waved him to be quiet. 'Here is a gun, as I have said. We are going to settle Thomas tonight, yes.'

Cleavely told the other about the girl and the old man, and the effect upon his employer was shattering.

'*Caramba*! That is the daughter of the fool Thomas! You let her go! Fool! Fool! Have I to pay you to make mistake? And Dekker — he make mistake, too! I trust him to work — I pay him well — he make mistake!'

'Guess the girl got away,' said Lebb calmly.

Swarthyface jutted his lips viciously.

'So it seems. Still we will force Thomas to give in. This is a very lonely house.'

'I don't know where the old guy fits in,' ventured Cleavely

'You know so little you are hardly worth your hire,' was the retort. 'I am not interested in old men. Bah!'

Swarthyface and Lebb were attired in belted raincoats and hats. With Cleavely in his not so immaculate suit they moved warily along the drive. They were sinister figures in the semi-gloom, and as they approached the house they ceased to speak and made signs instead.

Lebb had been instructed in the general scheme of things. He had to shoot, using a silenced gun, but Thomas and his daughter were not to be harmed.

There were lights in Carstairs when Swarthyface and his paid henchmen came close to the house. They lay and watched, like thieves in the night.

Figures moved across the uncurtained windows. Swarthyface saw Kennedy Balfour and his teeth bared.

'That young man I have promised to kill,' he said, and he raised his gun.

It was more of a gesture than anything else, because Kennedy soon moved away from the window and the range would have made such a shot very inaccurate. And Swarthyface did not want to reveal his presence so soon.

Inside the old house Kennedy, Clive and Dixon Thomas were doing their best to make Delia comfortable. She lay on a settee in the really comfortable lounge, and sipped strong black coffee.

Down in a cellar Dekker lay behind a strong door.

The little old man in fisherman's clothes sat blinking at the people round him. He had a scared look. His whole attitude was like a frightened animal whose sole idea is to bolt at the first opportunity He twiddled his greasy cap, and his bleary eyes darted from Kennedy to Clive and then to Delia and her father.

'It's most amazing how you escaped from that ghastly cell,' murmured Dixon Thomas for the fifth time. He smiled at the wizened fisherman. 'Your rescuer, Delia, has little to say, I'm afraid.'

'I don't think he understands very

well,' said Delia quietly. 'He was just as scared to find me as I was to see him. He did not want to come here, but I insisted. I wanted to reward him somehow.'

'Most amazing,' said Dixon Thomas again. He was half speaking to himself, going over the story Delia had told him earlier. It was a habit he had of musing over facts. 'There are some strange folk round these parts, I've always known, but to think of this old fellow actually living alone in the mouth of a cave — well, it is astonishing in these civilized days of 1946! But lucky for you my dear. Apparently he often wanders along the tunnels, and knows them all by heart. Well, well. And then again to think there is more than one iron gate down among those tunnels — but, of course, the smugglers must have used them as store-rooms. No doubt their mates were not too honest, and goods would have to be stored.'

Dixon Thomas was genuinely interested in the circumstances — apart from the fact that Delia was now safe. He had a slight interest in antiquities. He beamed at the old fisherman.

'So you had an iron key to fit the lock of Delia's cell! Most fortunate. Though come to think of it, you were actually in great danger, my dear, in wandering round those tunnels. We should have rescued you in any case.'

'I could hardly bank on that, Dad, at the time,' said Delia. 'This old man seemed like an angel. He stuck the key in the lock. I thought at first it was Dekker, and I wondered what was in store. Then I received another fright when the door was pushed open and no one entered. I thought I was going mad. I thought I imagined the sounds of the door opening, for you see I couldn't see anything. Anyway, the old fisherman was afraid of me and stood ready to run away. I still don't know how he knew.'

'Could have watched Dekker,' supplied Kennedy. 'Could have been hiding and Dekker would hardly guess.'

Clive grinned at the little old man.

'Yes, I say, how the dickens did you know Delia was locked in that damned place?'

Clive Fordingale's chirpy voice made the old man stare. He essayed a babble.

'Oi be seeing things, sir, all day, sir . . . in the dark. Oi can see, sir . . . see the lady and the gent . . . ha . . . ha ha ha . . . never see old Joe, sir.'

'So you hid some darned place,' interpreted Clive blandly. Clive took out a note from his case, gave it to old Joe. The old fellow stared at it for a long time.

'Perhaps it is years since he handled a note,' said Kennedy quietly. 'Far better to give him a bundle of food and suchlike. He may never go near a shop.'

'What do you intend to do with Dekker?' asked Delia. 'It seems incredible — he was quite a good servant. To imagine he worked for us all those months and all the time in the pay of Swarthyface! I don't know how you made him confess he was Swarthyface's man.'

'We had to use force,' said Kennedy, 'Do you feel better, Delia? Poor kid, I bet it was ghastly in that damned cell.'

Delia tried to control a shudder.

'I hoped that you would find me,' she said.

'We had another visitor — a tall, suave bloke. I had to hit him. Apparently he has gone back to his boss.'

At that moment a shot *phutted* through the air, smashing the window pane. The bullet missed everyone in the room and buried itself in the wall. Swarthyface had opened his campaign.

7

The Pretty Picture

Swarthyface had fired the first shot. He had crept closer to the wall of the old house, fired at the figure of Kennedy Balfour as he crossed the window. Garcia's shooting was like his nature — deadly but erratic. Swarthyface exclaimed in the gloom when he saw he had missed.

The next moment all lights in the lounge went out.

Swarthyface called Lebb quietly to his side.

'I do not think they have weapons — they are such young fools these Englishmen! Get Cleavely. We have them cornered in the one room. I will torture Thomas tonight. I will make him speak.'

But Duran Garcia had erred. He had forgotten that Dekker kept an automatic and that Kennedy Balfour possessed it now. True it held only six rounds —

Lebb moved swiftly to Cleavely.

'Come on. The boss is covering the window. We are going through the door.'

The main door yielded to Lebb's skeleton key in exactly five seconds. It was an old roomy lock, and the thin piece of stainless steel that Lebb inserted was better than the original key.

They went in at a crouch, running like expert gunmen. Their weapons were ready. The door of the lounge was soon found. It was closed. Lebb coolly crashed it open with his foot.

He was slightly disturbed when a shot spat close to his ear. Garcia was wrong! One of the fools had a gun. Lebb fired promptly at the direction of the shot. No cry of pain echoed in the dark.

Lebb and Cleavely were on either side of the lounge door. Lebb was cool and deadly. Cleavely was not so cool.

Lebb began to edge forward quietly. He wanted to find the electric light switch. It should be somewhere near the door.

His hand began to grope while his eyes searched the gloom like a cat. He was farther inside the room than Cleavely.

Inwardly he knew Cleavely to be a coward. Only a rat-like courage drove Cleavely into lawlessness.

Step by step Lebb came round the doorpost. There was no sound inside the room. He paused in his soft creeping progress to listen. Damned queer. He had trained himself to hear the slightest noise. There had been occasions before when his keen hearing had detected breathing on a similar episode to this.

Lebb's outstretched hand touched something. It was round and in the centre was a little trigger. The switch!

He pressed and at the same time dropped to his knees. He had no time to warn Cleavely, and in any case Cleavely could look after himself. He ought to guess what Lebb was after.

But Jonathan Lebb's cleverness was all in vain.

The room was empty!

A snarl came from the window.

Swarthyface appeared on the ledge. He was pushing up the already half-open sash window. His head came through. With incredible speed he eased his bulk into the room, and stood with revolver ready.

'Gone,' said Swarthyface ludicrously. 'Gone. How is this?'

The lounge, a wide old room furnished with big divans and high-backed chairs, was devoid of inhabitants.

'The door was closed,' jerked Lebb. 'I guess they didn't go that way.'

Swarthyface lurched round the room like a baffled gorilla.

'This is a ver' queer house — damned old, I guess. They have gone! Thomas, the girl, those two young fools — all the people I want! They have gone! How is that? Because there is some secret way out, I tell you.'

'Must be that,' grunted Lebb.

'You've got the chance to look for the pretty picture,' Cleavely pointed out.

Lebb went round the room tapping the walls with the butt end of his gun, but he achieved no tangible result. Cleavely examined the wide fireplace, tugging at various ornamental knobs.

'I wonder where Dekker is hiding?' growled Swarthyface. 'My hands would like to choke him for making fool mistake. He let the girl slip through his fingers — else how did she escape. He told me he had plans to hide the girl in some old tunnel. That was when I telephoned to him from Taunton. Now the girl is escaped! And Dekker! — where is he?'

'Maybe they tumbled to him?' suggested Cleavely.

'How? Dekker is in Thomas' employ for long time. He is trusted. When Thomas leave London, Dekker go with him. That is how I know where Thomas hide — in this old house! Thomas cannot escape me so long as Dekker work as his trusted servant. Dekker told me the girl return to London. I find her. But when she take the train again, I want to find out where she is going so I follow. She is only going back to her father at Carstairs, but then she meets this big young man.' Swarthyface glowered at the memory of his hiding. 'Him I will surely kill someday.'

'Let's search the house?' suggested Lebb.

'Keep your gun ready,' warned Swarthy-face.

'They'll be damned quick to beat me to the draw,' boasted Lebb.

'The big fellow is damned quick at many things,' said Cleavely nastily.

They went out into the passage. They switched on lights as they moved from room to room. Soon Carstairs was shining like an illuminated palace, except for the rooms, which were deserted and consequently had no electric globe. Lebb and Swarthyface looked into some of these rooms carefully, but they were devoid of the people they sought.

They went into the library. Swarthyface forced Dixon Thomas' desk, thrust his thick fingers through a few sheets of correspondence.

'Can't you find the pretty picture, boss?' asked Cleavely.

His curiosity concerning the pretty picture was growing stronger with the passing of time.

Swarthyface came over, pushed his yellow, fleshy face close to the other man's startled visage.

90

'Forget the pretty picture, my friend, It is not for you.'

'I'm only trying to help,' said Cleavely defensively.

'You are too damned curious to be helpful,' said the other deliberately.

'Do we get anywhere tonight or not?' interposed Lebb.

'There is nothing but mistakes!' raged Swarthyface. 'We have lost Thomas and the girl. Only through those two can I find the pretty picture. To ransack this house would take a week, and there is not time.'

Nevertheless, Swarthyface pulled down a number of books from the library shelves, looked at them for a moment and then flung them to the floor. He went round the shelves and when Cleavely began to copy his tactics, Garcia paused with a narrow, lowered expression.

'We are leaving this house,' he said abruptly. 'There will dawn another day, and if Dekker is alive he will return. I shall win in the end. Come.'

Cleavely smiled. Swarthyface, in his search of the books, had disclosed that the pretty picture was not a very large object if it could be hidden inside a book.

Lebb shrugged. He was a typical gunman and racketeer. So long as his boss paid, he could issue orders as he pleased.

They went round the house, came out among the outhouses and stables. Cleavely stopped beside a squat stone building and listened.

'There's someone in here!' he called sibilantly.

It was a case of the devil's own luck. The devil looks after his breed.

Lebb and Swarthyface, warily standing outside the heavy door, could hear distinct sounds as if someone was working hard inside the building. The noise was reminiscent of a rough file on wood.

Swarthyface discovered a lock on the door.

'Your key, my Lebb?' he said.

Lebb's piece of stainless steel was the product of a gentleman skilled in lock mechanism. Lebb prodded silently and the padlock opened.

They swung the door in about three inches, disclosing a dark smelly dungeon. The sound of rough filing stopped and there was silence for an appreciable time. Then a voice said:

'What do you want?'

Swarthyface gasped:

'Dekker!'

They went in, still cautiously. Swarthyface switched on his torch, with which he had provided himself before leaving Dartmouth town.

Dekker was attempting to escape from the stone building, and had actually begun sawing a small wooden window that was grilled with iron bars. He was using the rough edge of an old door hinge he had found. He had got out of his bonds by some clever means.

'Come along with us,' said Swarthyface harshly. 'And you can tell me how you failed.' He noticed Dekker's battered condition, his bruised lips and darkened eyes. 'So you have been punished already by the big young man!'

Dekker's expression became murderous.

'I'll gladly kill him. But they didn't get the girl. They forced me to show them where I'd left her, but I was damned surprised to find she was not there. Did you get her? How did you know where to look?'

'Thomas has his daughter back again,' snarled Swarthyface. 'How? We do not know. Cleavely saw her return with an old man — some sort of mad fisherman it seems. She is out of our hands, that is all I know.'

'Well, I only wanted to let you understand she'd got away before I showed them the place,' said Dekker sullenly.

'Come on. Let's get out of here!' snarled Swarthyface.

They trooped out into the dark night. A moon was rising, shedding a pale, wan light over the tracery of trees and the pile of Carstairs. The four men clumped silently to the road. Swarthyface halted, stood looking back at Carstairs with bitter glints in his black eyes.

'You have swallowed the fool Thomas and his friends,' he shouted dramatically. He was a Latin and loved a display. 'I could burn you down, but there is something I seek.'

Cleavely smiled sarcastically in the concealing darkness. Lebb waited patiently. Dekker was too busy massaging his chin to take notice.

'Come,' said Swarthyface, 'we have another day to make a plan that will not fail. Always there is another day, and that Thomas will learn to his sorrow.'

They had arrived near to Carstairs in a taxi, and Swarthyface, with his love of extravagance, had ordered the driver to wait their return. The car was some way down the road, and they walked on until Carstairs was out of sight. They rounded a bend and as they anticipated the taxi was still patiently waiting.

'So, we return, driver!' Swarthyface shouted boisterously at the figure at the wheel. 'We have talked with our old friends — now we go back to The Strong Arm.'

The driver had evidently felt the cold during his wait. His collar was upturned; his cap was wedged down to his ears. He merely nodded and got out to crank the ancient vehicle. So old was the car that it seemed a wonder it had negotiated the many dangerous bends and inclines leading up to Carstairs. As Duran Garcia and his associates climbed in, the vehicle creaked in every joint. But the four men did not bother about that.

The engine started with a splutter, and the driver came running back to his seat. It was such an ancient taxi that the driver was a remote operator separated from his passengers by a thick glass partition, and he was exposed to all the weather for the door was a mere panel across the gap leading to the road.

The driver let in the clutch, and the car moved off, slowly at first, and then with gathering speed. The road was a winding ribbon that dropped steadily for a mile or so into Dartmouth, and there were many awkward bends.

The driver took his cargo round two narrow bends with much swaying. On the right hand side of the bend the road dropped into an incline of wooded slope, and on the other side, houses made a boundary.

'He is in one big hurry!' grunted Swarthyface.

The taxi crashed on and in the moonlight the Dartmouth harbour appeared in sight. The water gleamed dully, and small yachts made black streaks on its surface.

The road suddenly curved into a hairpin bend. The car braked a little. On the right hand side the road was bordered by a wooden fence and beyond that a grassy slope descended straight into the water of the harbour.

As the car braked, the driver leaped out and flung into a stumbling run along the road.

The taxi plunged through the fence and down the grassy slope.

8

'The Best Laid Plans —'

Kennedy Balfour watched the ancient taxi plunge and tumble down the slope towards the water. Four men were in that car and he had made a deliberate attempt to severely injure them, or even send them to their deaths.

It had seemed the only way to put an end to the persecution of Dixon Thomas. The solution of Thomas' problems was the removal of his enemies. Perhaps the removal of Swarthyface alone might be sufficient, but it had been necessary to use whatever chances fate handed out.

And when Swarthyface had fired his shot in the lounge at Carstairs, Kennedy had immediately turned down the lights. He had told them all to crouch behind some solid furniture. Immediately Dixon Thomas had suggested they escape by means of an old secret panel that was a not too secret feature of a tall black oak sideboard. The panel led into a passage that was perfectly clean, having been whitewashed by the last occupants of the house and often shown as a showpiece of Carstairs.

They had thus hidden inside the passage in very much the same manner as the inhabitants of Carstairs in the past had often done, while their enemies searched fruitlessly for them.

Kennedy had decided to scout round, leaving Clive to ensure the others' safety. He had gone into the grounds, seen the lights in the other rooms. Suddenly he had decided to go for the police.

Kennedy saw that Swarthyface was largely dependent on bluff in his threats to Dixon Thomas. Perhaps Swarthyface could send Thomas to prison, but in that case he would surely lose his chance of forcing Thomas to give up his secret?

Yes, it was bluff. Of course Thomas could not face up to the threat. Prison was a horrible prospect when you actually faced up to it.

Kennedy had thought if he got police

to Carstairs. Swarthyface would run. And what was more Swarthyface would not dare show his face in Dartmouth again, unless he worked underground.

Kennedy had set off with this idea in mind — and it was only a half-formed idea — when he came across the taxi. Instantly he knew the carriage was waiting for Swarthyface and his pals. And instantly Kennedy conceived his idea. A drastic, grim idea, but it was obviously better than the police for if Swarthyface was dead, he could no longer threaten Dixon Thomas.

So Kennedy had bought the ancient vehicle from the old driver there and then on the spot. He had explained he wanted to play a joke on his friends at Carstairs, by surprising them later as he was driving them away,

A grim joke, Kennedy knew — He was wrong to do it.

The old fellow had fallen for the yarn Kennedy pitched, evidently glad to get rid of his ancient vehicle. Luckily Kennedy had enough money in his wallet to tempt him.

The taxi was now crashing and rolling

down the grassy slope, and at every collision pieces fell from it. Kennedy watched.

No one came out on to the road although there were houses nearby. He watched the doomed taxi rumble sickeningly towards the water. He wanted to see the end for himself.

But fate intervened.

The taxi headed straight for a clump of bushes and its headlong flight was checked. Still the vehicle had somersaulted once and the drag of the bush threw it over on its side.

The dust settled, and Kennedy watched silently. In the pale moonlight he saw a figure crawl from the wreckage, stand swaying for a moment and then help to extract another man. Then another man staggered out, after a jammed door had been wrenched away.

Kennedy waited. He saw the men work on the wreckage again, and within two minutes, just as a few curious local people appeared, they lifted out an inert body.

The body was laid on the ground, and it did not rise.

One of the gang had been injured, and

possibly was dead. Was it Swarthyface?

Kennedy could not tell. He lit a cigarette and walked away. He wanted to get out of his driver's uniform.

He walked swiftly to Carstairs, found everyone in the lounge again.

'Gosh, you've been a long time, old man!' greeted Clive. 'Did you come across old Sallowface?'

'We were getting anxious,' said Delia. Her blue eyes were smiling with the sudden lifting of worry. She had changed into a new blue frock, which to Kennedy's eyes was subtly restful. 'We guessed the gang had left Carstairs. Clive did a bit of scouting before we emerged from our retreat.'

'Let Mr. Balfour tell his own story,' interposed Dixon Thomas.

He knew the younger man was grimly moody.

Kennedy gave his yarn tersely.

'Swarthyface may be the one who came a cropper, but I'm not sure. Candidly I hope so.'

'So do I,' said Dixon Thomas. 'He is an evil man. He intends to do more evil in this world if he can get away with it. Death would stop him.'

'Unless his damned corpse continues the good work,' remarked Clive.

Delia had listened to the story with growing horror.

'If one of them has died, then the police are likely to get involved! If the gang talk, Kennedy could be arrested for murder!'

'Highly unlikely, I think.' Kennedy shook his head. 'The last thing Swarthy-face or his men would want is a police investigation. They'll probably report their crash as having been an accident.'

'It's still murder,' Delia whispered.

As Kennedy remained silent, his expression troubled, Clive suddenly spoke up. 'Have you forgotten how Swarthyface has already tried to shoot us? It was self-defence, if anything!'

Kennedy Balfour turned squarely to Dixon Thomas.

'Mr. Thomas, will you give me your complete story? What is Swarthyface after, and why can't you stop him by appealing to the police?'

'I can see that you have no other interest but to help me,' said Dixon Thomas in a low voice. 'Even after the experience of Dekker, I recognize a friend when I see one.'

Kennedy and Clive smiled at the other's earnestness

'Swarthyface is after something that will make him wealthy,' said Dixon Thomas abruptly. 'I have decided to tell you what that something is. But first let me tell you why Swarthyface can threaten me. I worked with him in Liverpool, as I have told you, and the work we were doing was illegal. We were forging bank of England notes,' said Thomas deliberately.

Delia flushed, turned unhappily away from Kennedy's side.

'Granted, I was compelled to work for Garcia, but nevertheless, I was a forger. Even at the beginning Swarthyface had power over me, for he had discovered I had forged a large cheque. Now, of course he has more power, though he is implicated himself.'

'What sort of work were you doing?' asked Kennedy.

'I was the key-man.' said Dixon Thomas. 'Can you not guess? I have exceptional ability as an engraver and a penman. My penmanship was my undoing in the first place, for if I'd not been so foolish as to forge that cheque, Swarthyface would have never compelled me to make his notes. At Liverpool I made an engraving — a plate as we called it — and this engraving was a perfect work of art, even if I do claim it. Swarthyface made a number of five pound notes from the engraving, and then I decided to run away.

'You must realise that crime and criminals were actually hateful to me, and there was Delia. If I was discovered — if the gang were caught, Delia would be dragged in the gutter. I decided to run away from Swarthyface and his organisation. Make no mistake, Mr. Balfour, Swarthyface had a clever organisation in Liverpool for the disposal of the spurious money, and the men are still ready to work for him. Lebb — one of the gangsters who called tonight — was one.

'I left Liverpool only by employing the

most cunning ruse. It would be a long tale, but to be brief I got away with Delia and we escaped to another town. For the next few weeks life was ghastly. I had the continual fear of the police and also the dread of running into Swarthy-face or his men. Well, one day I actually saw a man of his, but I was quick. He had not seen me, and so that night, not willing to take the chance of staying, Delia and I left for London.

'It was in London that I engaged Dekker. I realise now Swarthyface knew I was in London and sent Dekker to keep an eye on me. He was merely playing with me.'

'You haven't explained about the plate, Dad,' said Delia.

'Yes, yes I am coming to that. Kennedy, you will understand why Swarthyface pursues me when I tell you I escaped with the engraving — no one else could make another engraving like it — perhaps it might be a long time before I could execute another so perfect. I was determined not to leave this plate with Swarthyface. With it he could run off large numbers of five-pound notes, which were so perfect to defy even expert examination. Swarthyface had a plant in Liverpool — where I worked — and most probably it is still there awaiting the vital engraving. Also he had large stocks of special paper. He had just begun his preparations to issue the spurious notes on a large scale when I ran away with the engraving. Though, I'm afraid, he and I were responsible for issuing a good many notes. That is something that still torments me. I have made many mistakes.'

'What have you done with the engraving?' asked Kennedy.

'I brought it to Dartmouth,' said Dixon Thomas quietly. 'Do you understand the position? If I destroy the engraving Swarthyface will extract revenge by revealing me to the police. Even so by retaining it I draw Swarthyface's attentions. I will never let him obtain it, if I can possibly help. If he did get the plate, he would undoubtedly kill me for he fears I would give him away to the police. And I would do this sooner than see poor people robbed by issuing forged notes. They hit the poor hardest, you know. But so long as Swarthyface cannot find the engraving I'm afraid to approach the police. I would have to face a ghastly court trial. If only I could find some way of beating Swarthyface without talking to the police!'

And Dixon Thomas fell silent, deep in troubled thought.

'So that is the pretty picture about which Swarthyface sent his man,' commented Kennedy.

Dixon Thomas smiled faintly.

'A silly description of an engraving — but Swarthyface employed it to maintain an air of secrecy.'

'And if you destroy this engraving,' pursued Kennedy, 'Swarthyface will give you away to the police? Doesn't he run some risk himself in doing that?'

'He is very clever,' said Thomas. 'I have no doubt he would escape to Spain or Italy, where he is entirely at home. He would sell off his Liverpool plant, for he is not a forger himself — merely a criminal organiser. And without my engraving his plans cannot function.'

'Then the only hope for you is Garcia's death,' Kennedy summed up grimly. 'That is quite clear. Question — how?'

Clive furrowed his brow. His gingery eyebrows stood out ludicrously in the effort of concentration.

'What about a duel?' he suggested.

'Brilliant! With you, old boy?' asked Kennedy. 'What weapon would you choose?'

Clive missed the sarcasm.

'Quite a good idea, isn't it?' he said innocently. 'I think a duel with guns would fill the bill. No mess, you know!'

'Not the slightest,' said Kennedy, 'except when they pick you up. No, Clive, duels are off.'

'I have no right to drag you into this desperate business!' burst out Dixon Thomas. 'And Mr. Fordingale, I thank you for your duelling suggestion, extraordinary though it is.'

Clive gulped.

'Don't call me anything else but Clive, sir. I had thought of shortening my name to Ford, but seems too similar to the motor car, you know. People would ask me for catalogues, I should think!'

'I think I dragged Kennedy and Clive into this mess,' said Delia. 'I even offered Kennedy a weekly salary to be your bodyguard, Dad.'

'And a fine bodyguard I am,' muttered Kennedy, fumbling for his cigarettes.

'Pretty handy having a weekly salary,' remarked Clive. 'Though five pounds a week seems a little low to support a wife on, Kennedy.'

'What wife?' Kennedy stared.

'The one we used to jabber about when we were flying,' said Clive. 'The one you always said you'd like to meet after you were demobbed.'

'Oh, that. Oh, yes!' Kennedy seemed a trifle confused.

'Remember?' asked Clive,

'Er — yes.'

'She had to have hair and eyes like — like — er like Delia's,' said Clive, suddenly inspired.

'Have a cigarette,' said Kennedy ferociously. He came closer. He hissed in Clive's ear: 'And shut up!'

And with a cigarette stuck in his mouth Clive realised he had touched very tactlessly on several points.

He began to spout with sudden fierceness, with the definite intention of changing the subject.

'I say, Kennedy, give me a gun and I'll shoot Swarthyface. I'll do the damned job tonight, and we can go home, what? Nothing like home, even the Fordingale home,' and Clive ended with a cackle.

'We can't shoot a man in cold blood,' said Kennedy. 'And in any case, he may have come a cropper in the taxi — er — accident. We'll soon find out. In the morning the local paper will surely have an account of the — er — accident. So no shooting — as yet. I'm quite sure Swarthyface will come back to Carstairs for the engraving or the pretty picture, as he calls it. If he attacks again and is killed, the blame is off our hands,' finished Kennedy deliberately.

'I have hidden the plate in a fresh place,' said Dixon Thomas.

'Where is it hidden?' asked Kennedy.

Thomas shook his head.

'It may be better if I am the only one who knows.'

Kennedy shrugged.

Quite suddenly the bell on the main door rang. Kennedy rose coolly. 'I'll go,' he said.

He was away less than two minutes, and returned with another man.

'We have a visitor,' said Kennedy.

The man was Sid Cleavely. He was smiling suavely if a trifle uncertainly.

9

Dangerous Vigil

Sid Cleavely had been knocked about by Kennedy and had hated him for it. He still hated him. Actually Cleavely hated a lot of people, but if those same people could be used advantageously he was ready to turn on the mask of friendship.

Cleavely was ready to use the people he had expressly come to see. He announced his name to a surprised gathering.

'I've got a proposition to make,' said Cleavely. 'It's dangerous for me — doubly dangerous. You've only got Swarthyface to contend with, but I've got you lot and Garcia — and the police. That was a nifty trick you played on us, pal.'

'If you are addressing me, Kennedy Balfour is the name,' murmured Kennedy. 'And the chap on my right is Clive Fordingale. The others I should imagine you know.'

Cleavely was regaining his usual composure.

'I should have guessed when that damned taxi started to travel fast that something was wrong. You just got out in time, Mr. Balfour.'

'Did I?' Kennedy was thinking. Was this some trick? 'You seem to have escaped fairly well yourself.'

'Yeah, I was lucky. Dekker got his, though. He's dead.' He gave a twisted smile. 'And you can thank Swarthyface for keeping the police off your tail, Kennedy. He told them that Dekker had been driving, and lost control of that old vehicle.'

'I figured as much,' Kennedy commented. 'But he did that to help himself, not me.'

Delia had been listening intently. 'But the police would have checked on the licence number of the taxi, and tried to trace the owner. If they did that — '

Cleavely laughed shortly. 'They tried that, but got nowhere. The taxi had been unlicensed — the previous owner had left it in a scrapyard. Swarthyface told them

Dekker had acquired it from someone without his knowledge.'

Kennedy smiled to himself. No wonder that driver had agreed to sell him the vehicle, with no questions asked!

But Delia was still not satisfied that there was no danger in the police discovering Kennedy's involvement.

'Surely the police would have wanted to inform Dekker's next of kin? Inform his employer — ' her eyes widened at a sudden thought. 'He was employed by my father! Sooner or later they'll be calling here, and — '

Cleavely waved a hand impatiently. '*Swarthyface* was Dekker's employer — he was paid a regular salary, and he had no next of kin.'

Delia flashed an interrogative glance to her father. He smiled faintly, and shrugged.

'That explains a lot. Dekker always insisted that I paid him 'cash in hand.' He told me that he wanted it that way to protect some pension or other. I thought it odd at the time, but given my own position, I didn't inquire into it.'

Kennedy felt an intense sense of relief. He had not admitted that he had regretted his impulsive action, and was just as worried as Delia that the 'accident' might have brought the police investigating. 'OK — so we're all in the clear. Get on with your story!'

'Swarthyface and Lebb were taken to hospital for treatment, but I guess they'll be soon out. They were only cut a bit. That's how I was able to get here — while Garcia is in the hospital. I've got a proposition.'

'It's a trick!' cried Dixon Thomas.

'It's not a trick,' said Cleavely rapidly.

'What is the proposition?' asked Kennedy.

'I'll help you to get rid of Swarthyface,' said Cleavely. 'I'll help you to bump him off if you will pay well. I'm no fool, and I know that's what you want. Swarthyface is after something Mr. Thomas owns. There's something fishy about the whole racket, because why doesn't Thomas ask for police protection? So if Swarthyface is out of the way, Thomas is safe. That the set-up?'

'More or less correct,' admitted Kennedy.

'Now how would you get rid of Swarthy-face, Mr. Cleavely?'

The other smiled.

'Quite a few ways. You got to trust me and I got to trust you.'

'Why have you decided to double-cross your employer?'

Cleavely dusted his suit, which had been sadly treated that day, and reclined on the arm of a chair.

'I'm not so well in with Swarthyface as you think, and I want money. You'd pay good money if Swarthyface was dead, wouldn't you, Mr. Thomas?'

'It is murder,' said Dixon Thomas harshly.

'He'll get you if you're not careful,' sneered Cleavely.

'If Swarthyface returns to force me to his schemes, he'll probably be killed,' cried the other. 'But in that case we are justified — we are acting in self-defence.'

Cleavely lost his suavity.

'I'm offering you a chance to get rid of Garcia,' he shouted. 'He doesn't suspect me — I could get him easily. I want £1,000 for the job. Give me £500 now and the rest later when the job is done.'

'Don't believe it, Mr. Thomas! He'd buzz off with the £500 and Swarthyface would still be alive and kicking,' commented Clive.

Dixon Thomas was breathing hard. He could readily see that Cleavely's proposal was feasible. Here, with no difficulty, was the chance to rid himself of the man who was persecuting him. Could he take it?

'I — don't know — Kennedy — what should I do?' Dixon Thomas groaned.

In truth Kennedy Balfour was perplexed. The horrors of the recent war had loosened his rigid idealism, and he saw no wrong in removing so obvious a scoundrel as Swarthyface. Yet the man had the right to fight for his life cleanly. Going behind his back with a treacherous accomplice was pretty rotten. But if Swarthyface came back to Carstairs determined to kill him, kidnap Delia or steal Thomas' engraving — if he could find it — *then* the Latin could expect to face danger and death.

Cleavely offered to stab his boss in the back — probably literally.

Could the offer be taken?

'You can go to blazes, you swine,' said Kennedy pleasantly and suddenly. 'I admit the offer is tempting but it is the offer of a rat. We'll fight Swarthyface squarely, and what is more if he contemplates harming Miss Thomas or her father I shall have the pleasure of killing him with my bare hands.'

'You're making a big mistake,' choked Cleavely.

His confidence oozed away. He was beginning to realise he'd made an error of judgment. He was in a tough spot.

'You have made the mistake,' said Kennedy. 'Goodbye.'

'Think it over,' urged Cleavely, anxious to change their minds.

'I won't hit you,' said Kennedy calmly, 'because you came here under a white flag so to speak. But please do a bunk. You annoy me.'

'Buzz off, old boy,' murmured Clive.

Cleavely ran a hand through his black hair with a nervous movement.

'I'm getting out,' he said. 'You fools! Swarthyface will make it hot for you. I can tell you he has a scheme — *Aha* — '

A peculiar soft *phutt* sounded in the room coinciding with Cleavely's 'Aha.' Cleavely was sagging with wide terrified eyes. He clutched at a chair, pulled it over as he fell to the floor. He fell on his face and after two convulsive shudders lay still. A thin trickle of blood oozed from under him, on to the stained boards of the lounge.

Kennedy leaped for the light switch. Darkness fell over the room

'Get into the secret passage!' he ordered.

Someone outside had used a silenced gun on Cleavely, he knew. That someone could only be Swarthyface or Lebb. That had been another mistake of Cleavely's. Evidently Swarthyface and Lebb had got out of the hospital very quickly. It was quite clear. They had missed Cleavely, probably suspecting his actions.

Kennedy had Dekker's revolver. He went slithering to the window from which the shot had come. The pane was mostly missing — had been shattered earlier in the evening when Swarthyface had fired at Kennedy.

Kennedy thought he saw a movement

among the dark shrubbery, and he took a pot shot. The automatic barked and red flame stabbed the darkness. Kennedy waited for a cry of pain, and he grunted with annoyance when silence fell over the grounds.

'Damned quick those chaps!'

Kennedy did not stay at the window long. He did not want to offer himself as a target. He went over to the dark oak sideboard, rapped on the wood and fairly loudly:

'Are you there everyone?'

He heard Delia's muffled voice in reply.

'Stay put,' said Kennedy. 'I'm going out into the grounds just to see if I can catch those blighters. Not be long.'

He went out the main front entrance. He did not stand long on the steps, knowing better than that. He dived immediately for the cover of the shrubbery, and he had the automatic in one hand and his trigger finger was ready.

Kennedy scouted round to the shattered window of the lounge, and then made a detour round the wild shrubberies of Carstairs. He crept like a cat, and he stopped and tensed at the slightest sound. Mostly he was deceived by the wind among the laurel bushes and rhododendrons, which were growing to great heights. His search took him further and further away from the house.

It soon became obvious that the intruder had vanished. The longer he stayed, the more convinced was Kennedy that there had only been one gunman and that person, his job completed, had disappeared. After fifteen minutes silent scouting in the dark, Kennedy returned to the lounge. The lights were still out, though the fire glowed redly.

When he re-entered the lounge, Kennedy received a shock.

Cleavely's body had been removed!

Kennedy smiled grimly. The man's killer had concealed himself nearby, and seized his chance when Kennedy had moved away, searching the grounds. Glancing towards the window he saw that the entire pane had been removed.

Swarthyface was smart, he had to admit. He couldn't afford to have left a corpse with a bullet in it behind — that would assuredly have brought in the police.

Kennedy rapped on the old sideboard.

'All clear!' he sang out.

It was then he remembered something that struck him as funny.

When Delia and the others came out of the long sliding panel he immediately asked them about it.

'I've just remembered — so many events have happened — but what has become of old Joe? He was with us when we dived into the passage the first time.'

'We have wondered about that, too,' said Delia. 'In fact we meant to tell you when you returned from your taxi wrecking exploit, but I suppose we forgot, listening to your adventures. Old Joe was certainly with us, Kennedy, when we entered the passage the first time, but he never came out!'

Kennedy stared.

'We re-entered the secret passage to look for him and even shouted. But he's just disappeared,' Delia declared.

'He's not the only one!' There was surprise in Clive's voice. 'That body has gone too!'

Delia gave a gasp. She looked at Kennedy. 'But you said he was definitely dead!'

Kennedy told them what must have happened. 'You can be sure that Swarthy-face will know how to get rid of a body so that the police can never find it. And probably not for the first time, either . . . But I don't know what can have happened to Old Joe.'

Clive supplied a possible solution.

'The passage evidently has an outlet to the underground tunnels. Old Joe is probably familiar with every crack of this damned place.' Clive blinked. 'I — er — excuse my description, Mr. Thomas — assure you this is quite a fine old house. Should have a ghost, by jove! As I say, Kennedy, I imagine old Joe is encamped in his cave home by now, and probably glad to get rid of us.'

'This house was empty at one time,' stated Dixon Thomas. 'I should think the old fisherman had every opportunity to explore all the passages. We should be thankful for him,' Thomas concluded, looking at Delia.

Delia was glad to take her mind off recent horrible events, and she undertook to minister to her guests. She dived into the kitchen and Clive accompanied her this time as protector, and together they consumed a simple meal of Devon cheese and ham. Clive thoughtfully opened a jar of pickles, brought some in a cut glass container to the dining room. Dixon Thomas, driving his worries from his mind momentarily, brought out some sherry and filled their glasses. Clive saw there was whiskey, too. He felt suddenly happy and forgot they had just seen a man shot.

'You must make Kennedy and Clive at home, Delia,' said her father. 'Though without a servant it will be difficult. If we stay at Carstairs, we must get some more staff. Even with Dekker, it was difficult.'

Dixon Thomas sighed.

'We could find a place in Dartmouth,' suggested Kennedy.

'No, no. I will be more than pleased if you will stay, though perhaps you have business cares?'

'Not me,' grinned Kennedy. 'Thanks to

my late aunt. Clive hasn't a care in the world, business or otherwise. I suggest we hang on until we settle Swarthyface.'

But there was more than Swarthyface demanding Kennedy's attention, and as his eyes met Delia's she flushed, guessing.

'I am not a truly wealthy man,' said Dixon Thomas, 'though I did come into a considerable inheritance with the death of my wife. There was irony for you! At the same time that Swarthyface was forcing me to make plates — he had plans to forge hundreds of thousands of continental notes as well as English currency — my dear wife was killed in a road accident, Not long before that her brother had died, leaving her his estate. Ralph, her brother, was a different man to me. He had built up his wealth, and now that I possess it, I think I'd give a great deal away to be clear of Swarthyface.'

'Swarthyface will make a mistake and we'll use that mistake to beat him,' said Kennedy confidently, spearing a pickle.

Later Thomas poured out whiskey.

'We've got to have a guard tonight,' said Kennedy. 'Now if everyone trots off,

I'll stay up for the next four hours. After that Clive can relieve me. We've got the gun if it's needed. Remind me to get some more ammunition tomorrow, if we can, Clive.'

'But four hours is insufficient!' protested Thomas. 'You must allow me — '

'Clive and I are so underworked we can't sleep at nights,' said Kennedy.

They had to obey in the end. For the next four hours Kennedy sat up, gun in pocket, trying not to yawn. Then he went for Clive. For a sleepless person, Clive was doing very well at the occupation. He had been given an old bedroom, which was very near to the lounge and the other bedrooms occupied by Dixon Thomas and Delia.

'And don't go to sleep again!' warned Kennedy.

'That's all right. I can't sleep at nights,' said Clive mockingly.

But Clive pocketed the gun and strolled up and down the lounge until dawn tinted the sky.

'Damned good job, too,' growled Clive. It was about seven o'clock, and he felt the day was a sickly thing at that time.

But down on the seashore, about a mile away, a little man in fisherman's greasy clothes was already astir. He had made a fire in his cave mouth, utilising a precious box of matches and driftwood which yesterday's sun had dried.

Old Joe ate fish and bread, and seemed content. At least he was alone and not contemplating strangers who talked so quickly he could not understand their ideas.

The sun was rising, yet Joe had nothing much to do. His toilet entailed little time, for he merely scratched his head occasionally. His next meal apparently worried him not. He sat and contemplated the curling sea, and then after nearly an hour, he rose and went into the interior of his cave.

Old Joe left little at the cave mouth for anyone to steal. The remains of a fire, an old sack, a sheet of bedraggled newspaper — that was all. Yet a hundred feet inside the cave was a ledge that gave no hint that it concealed a natural safe. Old Joe climbed up quickly, pushed his arm deep into the narrow fissure and hauled up a small sack, which seemingly dangled down a hole behind the rocky face. The sack had a length of rope fastened to it, and this evidently held it from slipping beyond human eyes.

Old Joe climbed to a nook in the rock beside the fissure and sat holding the sack between his knees. He pulled out a few queer objects. He brought to light some nails, two rusty tins, a length of chain, a long rusty iron key, a piece of sailcloth, a scrap of plywood and lastly a small rectangular piece of metal.

Old Joe stared at the last object with great interest. It seemed he had no desire to gaze at his other treasures this morning. He fondled the plate, turned it round, gazed at its smooth side and then again at the engraving. What it represented he could only vaguely guess.

He muttered to himself. He was talking to himself about the rectangular metal plate he had found in his explorations.

He rubbed his fingers over the fine tracery of lines.

'Picture . . . ah . . . eee . . . ' muttered

old Joe. 'Ah . . . pretty . . . '

And then presently he placed his find back among the other treasures, tied the sack and lowered it into the hiding-place behind the rock.

And then grinning foolishly old Joe ambled away to the sea. He had been presented with a new find today and all sorts of things can be found if you look for them.

10

Unquiet Dreams

The bright spring morning was wearing on and Jonathan Lebb stood beside the ferry landing stage watching the gulls wheel and soar. Plenty of people were promenading the streets of Dartmouth, most of whom were visitors taking advantage of the fine weather.

Lebb was waiting for Duran Garcia. Lebb was hatless and was clad in his unobtrusive blue suit. He affected tan shoes and a black tie to a brightly checked shirt. It was a curious choice of colours, but Lebb was a curious man and a grim one.

He was smoking a cheap cigarette, staining his fingers an even deeper yellow. In his pocket his automatic lay, safety catch on. Lebb was not handling it.

The waters of the bay were rather choppy, for a slight breeze was coming in from the sea. And then Lebb saw Swarthyface, and he was faintly surprised, though his immobile face hardly moved

Swarthyface was standing on the deck of a small motor yacht. The yacht was approaching the quay somewhat lower than the ferry landing, and as Swarthy-face hailed, Lebb moved down to meet the incoming boat.

There were two men on board, Lebb discovered. He scrutinised them closely, which was merely his habit. One was a flannel-clad man of about fifty and the other a younger edition and obviously his son.

The boat tied up and the spluttering engine stopped. Lebb stepped on board as Swarthyface greeted him jovially.

'How would you like two weeks of sailor's life, my friend?' boomed Swarthy-face.

'Not a bad idea,' said Lebb calmly. He was wondering what Swarthyface intended.

'I have hired this fine boat,' said Garcia amiably. 'This good gentleman and his son, Mr. George Whiteman, senior and junior, as they say in the States, have loaned me their boat. What do you say to that, my Lebb?'

'Good idea,' repeated Lebb.

His lack of exuberance did not worry Swarthyface, who turned to the two strangers and shot out his fist. Very solemnly Garcia shook hands with Mr. George Whiteman and his son.

'Adios, my friends. I shall look after the boat as if she was my own.'

Whiteman and his son stepped ashore carrying their personal belongings. George Whiteman junior said:

'Queer bird. Hardly looks the sailor he claims to be.'

'Well, he's a foreigner, you know,' said the other. 'Anyway he's paid handsomely for the boat. The money is damned welcome, I can tell you. I wonder if I dare touch his deposit!'

Lebb went down into the cabin and looked round. There was room for eight people, he estimated, though his knowledge of boats was limited. There were three partitioned cabins with bunks, a small galley and one cabin, larger than the rest, contained a table and permanently fixed settees. Swarthyface came down after Lebb and smiled at his accomplice.

'What you thinking, my Lebb?'

'What's the idea?' asked Lebb abruptly.

'It is good idea that I have,' said Swarthyface. 'I tell it to you, my Lebb because you are the faithful one. You have worked with me a long time, and I trust you, not like that rat Cleavely!'

'Wonder just what he was proposing,' muttered Lebb.

'To work the double-cross!' said Swarthyface vigorously. 'He would play the traitor! Why else should he sneak away when we were being helped by the good hospital people. But you got him, my Lebb, and I thank you. You concealed his body well?'

'Let's just say it won't be found any time soon,' Lebb said callously. He rubbed his arm. Under his coat there were bandages.

'I'd like to get that big devil for what he did to us last night!'

'First we get Thomas or his daughter. Perhaps both — that would be the best idea. Then I can force him to make some new plates. Now that double-crosser Cleavely is no longer around, I can talk freely.'

'You haven't explained about this boat. What the hell you got in mind, boss?'

'It is simple. With this boat we take Thomas and his daughter away. Maybe a little voyage with us would make Thomas change his mind.' Swarthyface began to lose his amiability at the thought of his frustrated plans. 'The little fool! Here I have a fortune waiting to be earned and he defies me! Next time I will kill him if he refuses to do as I say. He will make a new plate — many new plates — or give me the marvellous one. Ah, Lebb, it made a pretty picture that plate!'

'How are you going to bring Thomas and the girl on to this boat? It's a good idea, if you can work it,' said Lebb.

'We will make plans,' said Swarthyface. 'And we shall live on the boat. We are leaving The Strong Arm. Too many peoples watch us, I think.'

Garcia had taken some instruction from the former occupants of the motor yacht, for he was able to start the engine and ease the craft away from the quay. He spun the diminutive wheel and opened the throttle to its maximum and the craft headed down the bay. In truth the *Firefly* — that was the boat's name — was not a fast craft, for her speed at full throttle was roughly six knots.

Swarthyface and Lebb spent the next hour getting the hang of their newly acquired possession, and then Garcia seemed satisfied. They slung out an anchor at a sheltered spot in the bay and began to talk of plans.

Meanwhile Kennedy Balfour and the others at Carstairs were still doing housework. Kennedy found working with Delia quite amusing, and he had given the girl to understand that he was definitely fond of making beds, washing dishes and preparing food. That this was an overstatement, Kennedy did not realize, such was his condition.

'It's no good,' said Delia at last. 'We've simply got to get help. I don't mind a little work, but goodness, look at my hands!'

Kennedy looked.

'Gosh, they're small, aren't they! They're pretty, too!'

'What — with those red marks!' demanded Delia.

Nevertheless, she had flushed. She looked at him, lips parted in a smile. She hardly realised how provocative she looked. Kennedy saw an extraordinarily pretty girl near to him, and a wisp of hair fell across her brow. She had an apron on and her arms were bare to the elbow and still wet with the washing up. Kennedy knew Delia would be a pretty girl in sackcloth.

'I — Delia — how long have I known you?'

'A couple of days,' said the girl after reflection.

'Gosh, seems that I have known you a long time and yet, of course, I haven't. Why we haven't even done a show — or anything people usually do,' Kennedy ended indignantly.

'We've been doing things some people never do.'

He smiled down at her. If Kennedy was tall, Delia was equally tall for her sex, and a good head above her father.

'We started all right,' murmured Kennedy.

'Did we? You mean Swarthyface — '

'No. Blast the man! Yet if he had not come along, I might never have met you.'

'Would that be such a serious blow?'

'You're kidding, Delia!'

'Such a vulgarism! Am I kidding?'

He caught her arms and said boldly:

'Yes. Delia — I — '

He bent down and kissed her. It was not a long kiss, but it was magical to both. He released her.

'Yes, we started all right when Swarthyface forced you to make love in the train.'

She said, 'Kennedy!' but he only grinned.

'I've got some work to do,' she said, and fled.

Later Kennedy met Clive. The latter, busy hauling coal from the cellar to the scuttles, stared.

'Hello, hello! Found a fortune — or is Swarthyface dead?'

Kennedy assumed a frown with an effort.

'Get on with the chores. Nothing has happened — nothing of importance, old boy.'

'When do we slug Swarthyface?' demanded Clive coarsely.

'When he pops up demanding a fight. What else? If he decides the game is too hot and runs off, then we have won.'

'Rather negative, isn't it?'

'It is,' admitted Kennedy. 'For the simple reason I don't believe Swarthyface is finished yet.'

'I should damn well hope not. I haven't got into my stride. I say, Delia's a frightfully pretty girl, isn't she?'

Kennedy admitted the fact calmly.

'Pity you're around, old boy,' said Clive regretfully. 'With my permanently startled look, I don't stand a chance. I know I've got a permanently startled look because a girl once told me so.'

And Kennedy frowned in earnest.

He went to the library, found Dixon Thomas at his desk staring moodily into space.

Kennedy sat down in a huge leather chair.

'I've got a suggestion to make, sir. Do you think the best plan is to stay at Carstairs?'

'Stay — stay — I beg your pardon, Kennedy. I wasn't listening.'

'I suggest we move to one of the big hotels in Dartmouth and lock up Carstairs. Here we are exposed to every move of your enemy, but living at a hotel Swarthyface would be stumped. He could not make raids on you. He would have to watch for other people, and he would be rather restricted.'

'Seems quite a good idea,' responded Dixon Thomas. 'But why Dartmouth? I merely bought Carstairs because it was lonely, and I thought Swarthyface would never find me. Why should I not run off to another lonely spot, and without Dekker to spy on me, I might be safe for a long time.'

'Swarthyface would find you,' said Kennedy. 'There is just as good a case for standing and fighting him. Why not try my suggestion and move to a hotel? That would solve the servant problem, at least.'

Dixon Thomas sat for less than a minute.

'You are right, Kennedy. How I wish I had your drive and determination. Thank goodness Delia is more like her mother than me.'

It was settled. There was a great deal of bustle as Carstairs was tidied and made ready to lock up. Delia and her father collected their personal belongings, such as they would need, and Kennedy rang up a Dartmouth hotel.

There was a hitch. The first hotel was booked, but the manager was very anxious to please. He insisted that Kennedy should let him make inquiries on his behalf.

'There is not much accommodation in the town,' said the manager pleasantly. 'But allow me to make inquiries. I'll find you a place, I promise you.'

'Helpful chap!' murmured Kennedy. He lit a cigarette and waited patiently.

Ten minutes later the 'phone rang and Kennedy began to speak to his helpful hotel manager.

'The Green Dragon has rooms and I sincerely recommend them. I have spoken to Mr. Widdicombe for you, not without a lot of other inquiries,' and the manager chuckled. 'However, I'm so sorry I could not accommodate you, but you'll be very comfortable at the Green Dragon. It is one of the best licensed hotels in the town.'

Kennedy thanked him, and got through to the Green Dragon.

A suite of three rooms and bathroom was booked. Then Kennedy rang Dartmouth for a taxi.

The taxi arrived after what seemed a long wait. Kennedy was ready to talk strongly to the driver, but he forgot his annoyance ultimately.

Delia and her father climbed in and then Kennedy and Clive. Luggage was strapped on the grid at the rear of the car. The car set off, Carstairs, locked and barred, receded behind its leafy surroundings.

They had hardly reached the main road when there was a sudden, dramatic change.

The driver, plain and unobtrusive in his white raincoat and peaked cap, turned round. The car was modern, and his seat was not partitioned from the other seats. He turned, and in his hand was a pistol. The car squeezed to a standstill.

The driver pressed the trigger of his pistol, and a soft hissing spray enveloped his surprised passengers. The odorous liquid flew to the passengers' nostrils, and they gasped for breath.

Kennedy jerked forward, even as his brain clouded. He seemed to be fighting a drugged feeling. His senses were reeling . . .

He drove back one spasm of darkness with desperate effort of will-power. If he could — only — get — to — the man —

The others were in a similar plight. Delia was the first to go under.

She slumped in her seat, unconscious. Then Dixon Thomas, gasping at the spray-filled air, went limp.

Clive and Kennedy were harder nuts to crack, but the end was inevitable. The driver, grinning with triumph, had filled the air with the drug. The two young men fell back and their eyes closed,

Even then the driver made sure of them. He looked at their eyes under the eyelids. He slipped back to his seat and started the car.

Under his breath he was cursing his respirator, but he did not attempt to remove it.

11

The Trail Widens

When Kennedy Balfour opened his eyes he thought for a bewildering thirty seconds that he was at his dentist. Then, with the damnable realisation clearing his mind, he jerked his body into motion. The movement was abortive from the start, for as the dope cleared quickly, he discovered that he was bound hand and foot. His instinctive jerk to action was frustrated.

Kennedy cursed. Vivid pictures of the white-coated driver pointing his spray pistol . . . he, Kennedy, striving to reach the man . . . Delia going limp . . . the smell of the sickly stuff — all these mental pictures flashed through Kennedy's brain with the speed of light.

Delia! With a mighty curse at his uselessness, he struggled to a sitting position, looked round grimly. He saw

Clive by his side and his friend was slowly wriggling and muttering. The drug was apparently clearing from Clive's head also.

Kennedy looked up and around him, saw several things in one grim photographic impression. He saw Lebb. He had seen Lebb before in the driving mirror of the old taxi just before he had plunged them over the cliff. Kennedy guessed that Lebb had been the man with the spray gun, and the thought filled him with fury. Lebb was not wearing his white raincoat, but was clad in a blue suit and tan shoes. Oddly, he was also wearing tight-fitting gloves. As Kennedy stared, Clive struggled to a sitting position, looking more than ever as if he'd seen an apparition. Kennedy essayed a slow grin and the gesture cooled him.

'What have you done with Delia?' asked Kennedy quietly.

Lebb did not smile.

'She is with the boss. We've got Thomas, too. And this is where you two fade out, chums. Get me right — this is Garcia's idea, though he cannot be here to see you. Personally I'd sooner use this.' And Lebb patted a heavy object in his jacket pocket.

'Perhaps. Has Swarthyface another idea?'

'Yeah, This is it,' said Lebb indifferently, and he indicated a heap of shavings in a corner. They were wood shavings, and Kennedy noticed for the first time that he was inside a shed, which was apparently a carpenters' workshop. Beside the shavings stood a two-gallon can of petrol. Kennedy understood Swarthyface's idea in seconds, and the reason why Lebb was wearing gloves.

'Garcia would like to see you guys roast,' said Lebb calmly. 'But he's got other things to do at the moment. Anyway, his idea is you'll die slowly. See? You'll have time to appreciate the idea.' Lebb gave one of his rare smiles. He took a short stub of candle from his pocket, set it among the shavings. Before lighting the wick, he opened the petrol can and liberally soaked the shavings and the surrounding woodwork of the shed.

'Nobody comes here,' said Lebb. 'And

you needn't bawl because this old boathouse is miles from anything.'

Lebb carefully lit the candlewick. Even so with the air smelling of petrol fumes there was danger that the roasting operation might start prematurely. But the candle — hardly an inch in length — began to burn. Lebb went immediately to the door.

'So long, pals. See you someday — in hell!'

Then he was away.

Kennedy heard Clive whistle cheerfully, and for a moment the noise irritated him. Then he gave a disgusted sort of grin.

'Fine bodyguard we are. What beats me is how Swarthyface worked the trick. How did he know we had sent for a taxi?'

'Haven't the foggiest, old boy.' Clive was grunting as he twisted his tied wrists. 'It would seem that old Funnyface is cleverer than we thought.'

'He's got Delia,' gritted Kennedy. 'Damn him!'

Behind his back his hands were bound with new manila rope, and the bindings would simply not give no matter how hard he strained. For a second or two, Kennedy contemplated rolling over to the flickering candle and attempting to blow it out, but he soon saw the candle was perilously balanced. It was stuck to a piece of a cigarette carton and the carton was lying on top of a wadding of petrol-smelling wood shavings. If he once touched this uncertain hook-up, the thing would probably fall among the shavings and then . . .

It seemed impossible to approach by rolling and wriggling and still guarantee the candle staying steady until he could blow it out.

Of course, in any case it was merely a matter of minutes before the candle burnt down and ignited the shavings. So what . . .

Lebb had locked the door on going out. Lebb had seemed pretty sure nothing would spoil his plan.

Kennedy used his muscles to strain at his wrists. Had it been old rope there would have been a certain amount of stretch. Lebb evidently knew better than to use old rope. Lebb, it seemed, had had some experience.

The candle had a queer fascination. Kennedy found himself watching its slow curving flame while he strained futilely. Red-hot frictional pain rasped at his wrists, and he began to perspire.

'We're complete fools!' Kennedy spat disgustedly. 'My God, what will Delia think of us!'

'Very little little, old boy,' commented Clive. 'In a minute or two it will be rather hot in here. I say, what would I give for a damned old foam-extinguisher!'

'I got you into this blasted mess!'

Clive worked his way round to Kennedy and was able to place his bound wrists so that Kennedy could tackle them with his teeth.

Kennedy Balfour had good strong teeth, but he groaned when he saw Clive's wrists had been bound and tied with at least four separate knots. The shed would be in flames long before he could tug half the knots free.

'No good,' muttered Kennedy. 'I'm going to try for that candle. There's a ticklish chance of extinguishing that wick

— but my God! — what a chance. I'll probably knock the thing over.'

Clive licked his lips. 'That'll only anticipate the bonfire by a minute or so,' he said dryly.

Kennedy rolled once, steadied and looked at the candle. It seemed to blink redly at him. He prepared to roll again.

'Oooh! Are you playing at gangs?' said a sudden childish treble.

Kennedy jerked his head. His eyes darted incredulously round the shed. At one corner a plank had been slid aside showing white daylight and a small boy in short trousers and zip jacket.

'Quick! Come here!' roared Kennedy.

'Did the other gang get you?' asked the small boy excitedly.

Kennedy almost stuttered. Clive was still gaping.

'Come here son. See that candle? Can you blow it out without upsetting it? For the love of Mike don't upset it!' Kennedy rapped the words like pistol shots.

The boy crept in. His blue eyes gleamed with true zest for adventure, but his ignorance that there was real danger made Kennedy feel distinctly nervous.

'I'm in a gang,' began the boy. 'We — '

'Listen son, there's petrol on those wood shavings. If that candle touches the stuff — !' Kennedy almost choked. 'Now for God's sake be careful. Blow that candle out, son. Blow it out!'

'Will you tell me all about your gang — '

Clive's eyes were nearly popping out of his head.

'We'll tell you anything!' he said.

'I like to come here,' confided the boy. 'When I get my gang I'll make this my headquarters. Good job I knew how to get through the loose plank, because your gang would have lost.'

'Sonny — the candle!' Kennedy repeated urgently.

The flame seemed to be swimming in a liquid stump. Kennedy had a new anxiety. He did not want to drag the youngster into danger.

However if the boy moved quickly and carefully —

The small boy took his duty seriously and stealthily approached the candle set on its piece of cardboard. It was a tense period, and then it was over. The boy, walking carefully, leaned over and blew sharply.

The candle was snuffed, leaving only a wisp of smoke.

'Have you a penknife, son?' asked Kennedy. 'We're tied — can't get free.'

'I've a good penknife,' boasted the boy. 'What have you got to do now that you're free?'

'When we're free we've got to rescue a lady,' said Kennedy grimly,

'A beautiful one,' corrected Clive with a grin.

'Oh, girls are no good in gangs,' said the boy disdainfully.

The youngster's penknife was badly in need of a new edge, despite his boast that it was a good one. Cutting the rope was a slow job, but eventually Kennedy was free. Kennedy took the penknife and sawed through Clive's bonds.

Then they stood up, rubbing their wrists.

'If Swarthyface had listened to Lebb, there'd have been no comeback for us,' said Kennedy. 'Here you are, my boy

— here's ten shillings. You're actually worth a great deal more, but you might plunge into riotous living if we hand you more. What will you do with this note — buy a savings certificate?'

'No, sir. I'll go the pictures — I go to the pictures twice a week.'

'To see the gangsters, eh?'

'Yes, sir. There was some gangsters at work last night,' said the boy darkly. 'A motor car crashed over Dipper's Hill and a guy was killed. It's in the papers. I read it. The papers say it was an accident but I think there's something queer — that's what my Dad says.'

They got out of the shed and departed from their juvenile rescuer. Presumably they had met a future detective or crime lawyer, but Kennedy and Clive had not time to waste.

Kennedy and Clive found that the old boathouse that was to have been their funeral pyre was a long way out of Dartmouth. The shed was set among trees and only a few yards from a shallow creek which flowed into the sea not far distant.

They walked briskly out of the clump of trees and reached a road. They set off for the town.

'Now what?' asked Clive.

'Find Swarthyface,' was the reply. 'If he is hanging round Dartmouth, we'll see him. After all, we're only about ten minutes behind Lebb, and he must be returning to his boss. Now Swarthyface and his chum were hanging out at The Strong Arm — a pub.'

'They couldn't take Delia and Thomas to the pub,' interposed Clive.

'I don't suppose so, but we can start by making inquiries at The Strong Arm. We've got to start somewhere. Come on, run!'

They broke into a steady trot along the flinty road. They passed a few people strolling the roads for pleasure, and Kennedy and Clive received their quota of curious looks.

'That damned taxi was slow in arriving at Carstairs,' said Kennedy suddenly. 'Obviously Lebb got to know we were leaving Carstairs — he isn't a thought reader, so he learnt the news somehow.

He turns up in a taxi — questions are how did he learn we wanted a taxi and what happened to the driver of the firm I rang up?'

Clive came up with answers as if inspired.

'The secret, old boy, lies with your helpful hotel manager. Now listen to this. The helpful one makes inquiries at various hotels and inns, all on your behalf. Supposing he rang up The Strong Arm? The manager of The Strong Arm might easily pass on the news to Swarthyface and Lebb — I admit I don't know why, but perhaps old funnyface made it his business to be extra pally with mine host. The rest follows easily. Obviously if the occupants of Carstairs were leaving, they'll want a taxi. Lebb undertakes to watch for taxi leaving for Castairs. Admittedly, again, I don't know how he wangled it, but the blighter evidently got hold of the taxi you rang for. The dope pistol is perhaps his own little gadget — part of their stock in trade. So there you are!'

Clive had to gasp for breath. Keeping

up with Kennedy's huge strides and talking were a task demanding too much.

'A good effort, Clive,' said Kennedy. 'You can't deduce the whereabouts of Delia and her father from the fact that Swarthyface is busy and Lebb cannot be far away?'

They were approaching rows of white villas lining the road, and they passed on and still Clive could not supply an answer to Kennedy's question.

'Maybe Swarthyface is getting ready to run off with Delia and her father!' suggested Clive. 'We'll have to look for a big car. Better still — go round to the garages and ask if anyone has bought or hired a car.'

'We'll have to bear one definite thing in mind,' said Kennedy. His words came easily despite his steady pace. 'Thomas told me he had hidden the engraving in a new place, yet the new place is bound to be in Carstairs. If Swarthyface discovers the place he'll go to Carstairs to seek the plate. We'll have to watch for him.'

'And if Thomas took the plate with him in his bags?'

'I don't believe he did,' said Kennedy. 'But if he did it is one for Swarthyface. That is not all he wants of Dixon Thomas though. He'll force him to make engravings of continental currency. I can see that Garcia is out for big profits. And to force Thomas, he'll use Delia.'

The grim look on Kennedy's face prompted Clive to say quietly:

'You think a great deal of Delia, Kennedy.'

Kennedy paused to punch the other's arm lightly.

'I'm going to ask her to be my wife,' he said, 'when I've smashed Swarthyface.'

'And I'll be best man,' retorted Clive with a huge grin. 'But first, we've got to do for Swarthyface before the day is out!'

They soon found The Strong Arm. The inn lay down a cobbled alley and Kennedy ducked through the low door and into the bar. The place was still open and a number of customers were drinking beer and cider. Clive and Kennedy came to the counter, and the individual behind the pumps gave them an interrogative look.

Kennedy went straight to the point. The individual forgot his beer pumps, and his plain face took on a frightened expression.

'You've got a bloke staying here called Duran Garcia — a foreign-looking man. With him is a man called Lebb. Where are they now?'

Kennedy was more than forthright; he was blunt. The Manager of The Strong Arm stammered. As Swarthyface had remarked, he was an ex-crook and a timid one. He didn't want any trouble. As it was he could speak truthfully.

'They've left. They took their luggage this morning. I don't know where they are now.'

The manager was a Londoner, judging by his speech. He had the city man's ability to judge quickly and he had guessed that Kennedy was in a cold anger. He did not know anything about Kennedy Balfour, except that he was towering above his counter, and he wanted him to go quickly.

'You're quite sure you don't know where they are? You know about whom

I'm talking — Garcia, the Latin with the figure like a gorilla and black hair and eyes.'

'I know — I know. I tell you, he's left!'

Kennedy reluctantly took his bands off the bar counter.

'No go,' he said to Clive. 'Come on.'

'I say, I think I know the chap you want,' said a voice.

Kennedy glanced at the speaker. He saw a man of fifty clad in flannels and a jacket. Next to him was a younger edition who in every feature proclaimed himself to be the other's son. They were both drinking cider.

'My name's George Whiteman,' said the speaker. 'If I'm not mistaken I loaned a motorboat to a chap who answers to your description. Swarthy-looking sort of bloke — I forget his name dash it, I don't believe he even told me his name! The amount of money he offered me rather led me to overlook things.'

'He called his friend Lebb,' said George Whiteman junior calmly. 'I'm not quite sure that I like the pair, Dad.'

'My dear boy, that has nothing to do

with it. I needed the damned money — and — er — ' Mr. Whiteman coughed, and looked at Kennedy somewhat shamefacedly.

'Yes, sir; they borrowed our cabin cruiser, *Firefly*.'

12

Take to the Water

When Delia Thomas eventually opened her eyes she found herself staring at a curious wood ceiling that seemed to be only a foot or so from her face. She felt rather sick and the surface on which she was lying seemed to be rising and falling. She lay for almost a minute with her eyes wide open before the image of the man with the spray pistol came into her mind.

And then with a leap of her heart she realised everything. Duran Garcia had kidnapped her and undoubtedly held her father. She struggled to a sitting position and, staring ahead, saw she was inside the cabin of a small boat. She was sitting on a bunk.

She slid to the floor unsteadily. Somewhere a motor was vibrating and the craft was slicing through choppy seas. She had to hold on to the bunk while she adjusted herself to the feeling,

Then the next instant her eyes fell to another bunk and saw her father lying. He was still under the drug. Delia went over and tried to waken him. Her efforts were partially successful, for Dixon Thomas opened his eyes drowsily and then shut them again. Presently after five minutes, during which time Delia patted his hands and smoothed his brow, he came round.

'Delia — where am I — Delia, what has — oh, I remember!'

'We're in a motorboat,' said Delia. 'Oh, it's quite clear — Swarthyface has got us, That was one of his men driving the taxi.'

'Probably Lebb,' said Dixon Thomas. 'An ingenious device — that dope pistol. We should have taken more precautions.'

And then the same thought struck them and they both began to speak at the same time concerning the puzzling affair of the taxi. How had Swarthyface known they'd rung for a taxi?

Delia and her father had no time to think about the matter, for the cabin door opened and Jonathan Lebb walked in. His black sombre eyes were narrow.

Dixon Thomas spoke bitterly.

'So we meet again, Lebb. Still serving your master? You were very clever with your pistol.'

'So you've come round,' commented Lebb. 'Listen, Thomas. Why do you buck against the boss? If you worked for him, he could make you dough. He's going to make you spill the beans about the plate.'

'I do not want his money,' snapped the other. 'I want peace of mind,' and Dixon Thomas almost quavered.

'What have you done to Kennedy and Clive?' Delia asked the question with a tremor of fear at the answer she might receive.

'They are cinders now, I guess,' said Lebb indifferently.

Delia went white and inside she had a ghastly feeling of horror. And then sheer fury filled her. Her arms flew up to Lebb's throat.

The gangster jumped back. A gun appeared magically in his hand while his eyes smouldered.

'Keep back, sister. Thomas, call her off

or I'll slug her and tie her up.'

But Delia, recognising the hopelessness of resistance, fell back limply her rage almost giving way to despair.

'What has happened to Kennedy and Clive?' she repeated

'I've told you — I burnt them! It was Garcia's idea. They were getting in his way. I would have used the gun.'

'You callous swine!' shouted Dixon Thomas.

Lebb gave his thin grin.

'Stow it.'

Suddenly a head appeared round the cabin door. It was a big black head and the amiable grin was Swarthyface's.

'My Lebb, please to take the wheel. Now that my friend Dixon Thomas and his pretty daughter are our guests and wide awake, I shall talk to them. So.'

Lebb disappeared, and two seconds later Garcia came down into the cabin.

'Ah, my dear friend, Thomas! You are on my boat — *Firefly* — what a funny name! It is a long time since we had talks.'

'You have murdered two friends of

mine!' said Dixon Thomas in a low voice. 'Those two young men — my God — it is terrible! I shall never do your bidding, Garcia. Never!'

Swarthyface lost his smile, and his pendulous lower lip jutted nastily. His eyes glinted like black crystals.

'You will do just as I desire, for have I not your lovely daughter to keep us company? This time she is in my care and not under the blundering hands of hired underlings like Dekker. I shall see that there is no escape. And you, my friend, will make me some pretty pictures.'

Dixon Thomas trembled helplessly. What use was it to defy this brute? What was the good of brave words when all the time Swarthyface held the trump cards.

'Where is the plate? The Bank of England five-pound engraving?' elaborated Swarthyface.

'I will not tell you,' stammered Dixon Thomas.

'Damn!' shouted Swarthyface. 'You will tell me. If you do not I will give Lebb orders to punish your little girl. You will not like that. Where is the plate? You brought it to the old house I know.'

The other remained silent.

'I will be very, very patient,' said Swarthyface. 'I a patient man — how else do I control my organization? I need the plate now. Now, do you understand? I have men and plans waiting for that one plate and you — ' Swarthyface scowled — 'you stop everything with your obstinacy.'

Dixon Thomas looked helplessly at Delia.

'He wouldn't dare torture me,' she said defiantly.

'That is a right word, Miss Delia,' Swarthyface declared. 'Lebb will torture you. Better persuade your father to be reasonable. And please hurry!'

The last three words were simply hissed. It was obvious that Swarthyface's patience was not great.

There was silence on the part of the two people facing him. Silence — because Dixon Thomas was thinking grimly. Silence — because Delia would defy until the bitter end.

'Lebb!'

At the enraged shout Lebb's thin, peaked face shot round the cabin.

'Come down and do what is the dirty work for me!' bellowed Swarthyface. 'Tie the wheel. Come and show Thomas how you can torture!'

Lebb came in grinning and he brought out his automatic. He emptied the shells into his hand.

He went immediately to Delia and brought the butt end of the gun across her knuckles. Before Delia could back away he had rapped her knuckles with such force as to bring the tears to her eyes.

'Just a sample,' said Lebb. 'And now this!'

He used the butt end to hit Delia violently on the shoulder. The heavy metalled gun dug into a most tender part of her muscles causing agonising pain. Delia tried to kick out, but Lebb, grinning thinly with amusement, side-stepped and brought his gun down on Delia's other shoulder.

Dixon Thomas jumped to Lebb in a blind rage.

'You swine! You swine! Leave her alone.'

Swarthyface wrapped his great arms round Thomas, and the small man was like a helpless child.

'I've got other ideas with a gun butt, boss,' drawled Lebb. 'For instance, I could spoil this dame's beauty in five seconds. The butt end in her face — like this!'

He made a movement and to Delia, choking with a sickening combination of fear and anger, it seemed that he was about to strike her face.

But the movement was only a feint. Lebb was demonstrating his skill, and was proud of it.

'And why don't you show me?' chuckled Swarthyface. 'Go on — hit her face!'

'No! No!'

Dixon Thomas shouted desperately. He was beaten. Such ghastly sufferings could not be inflicted on his only daughter.

'I'll tell you where to find the plate,' he said quickly. 'And I'll work for you if you allow Delia her freedom.'

'Good. Work for me, my Thomas, and your pretty girl will come to no harm.

Where is the plate?'

Dixon Thomas drew in his breath. He had fought to keep the engraving from falling into the other's hand, but now he was beaten.

'I hid the plate in the tunnel cellar in which Delia was made prisoner. I wrapped the plate in canvas and stuffed it in a corner of the cellar. I had vague plans of using gunpowder to blow in the roof, if it ever became necessary.'

Swarthyface smiled.

'So the pretty picture is still under Carstairs. No matter — I shall find it. I knew of course, you had not taken the plate with you when you left Carstairs, for we searched through your luggage.'

Swarthyface gave orders to Lebb.

'Turn the boat round and make for the shore again. I think if we anchor on a stretch of the coast that runs about a mile from Carstairs, we'll be able to save time.'

Lebb disappeared to do his employer's bidding. Swarthyface grinned at Delia and Thomas.

'In the meantime you will be locked up in this cabin. You needn't look for weapons, for you will find none. Later, Mr. Thomas, you will accompany me to the cellar in the tunnel, and I shall carry a gun. You will play no tricks, for Lebb will remain on board the boat with your pretty daughter.'

And then Delia and her father were alone. They heard a lock click as Swarthyface closed the cabin door.

'Delia, did he hurt you, my dear?'

She smiled bravely.

'It wasn't much after all, Dad,'

'If only I were a young man. I would kill Swarthyface! But I talk like a fool!' groaned her father. 'I will have to submit to Garcia. We are beaten. I shall show him where to find the plate and I shall make him more plates and perhaps he will let you free to take up a new life.'

The last two words made Delia choke. A new life? They held a horrible significance now that Kennedy was dead, for a lovely thing had grown between them that had promised a new life — a life they could share.

And now Kennedy was dead, and Clive, too. It was too awful to think about.

Delia stared through the small port-holes for a while and saw they were rounding a prominent jutting cliff and drawing nearer to the coast. She guessed the boat was approaching the nearest sea-point to Carstairs.

To Delia the whole chain of events since learning of Kennedy's death was like a fantastic film. She had to force herself to believe they were happening. She felt numb horror every time she thought of the man she knew now she loved. Had loved — for Kennedy was dead. Once, while staring white-faced through the porthole, a sob escaped her, and her father came and placed an arm round her shoulder.

'Don't worry, my dear. Everything will be all right.'

'I — I can't help thinking — of Kennedy. They've killed him. Oh, and I loved him!'

And then Dixon Thomas said grimly:

'Perhaps it is the truth but that young man will take a great deal of killing. And that goes for his friend, too.'

There was a sudden wild hope in

Delia's heart. It was the same faint hope women all the world over cherish when their loved ones are in danger.

'Do you think he could have escaped — do you, Dad? I believe he could! I believe he could!'

And her eyes were shining.

In his heart Dixon Thomas hardly held the same confidence. He knew Lebb had spoken too positively for there to be any mistake.

But he said nothing, for it was impossible to destroy Delia's new-found hope.

The *Firefly's* engine thudded away with monotonous regularity. Looking through the porthole Delia saw the land was plainer and barely half-a-mile distant.

The propeller threshed until the boat came within a few yards of the shore, and there Lebb dropped an anchor and stopped the engine. He found he was becoming quite a sailor.

The cabin door opened and Swarthyface entered.

'And now my Thomas we go to seek the plate that brings us much money!' He was in a jovial mood, but there was no one present to appreciate him. 'Come.'

'I'll be quite safe, Delia,' said Dixon Thomas. 'Stay quiet until I return.'

'She will be quiet, I promise you,' chuckled Swarthyface. 'Lebb will see to that. But have no fear of Lebb, little one. He is good, is Lebb. A fine man. Why, I have the idea — why don't you marry him, eh?'

Delia gasped in horror, and Swarthyface leered. At that moment he looked as ugly as an ape with his huge jowls und neck, and thick black hair.

'Come my Thomas, you show me the tunnel and no tricks. I have gun, see!'

And Swarthyface displayed an ugly automatic.

Within a few minutes they left the cabin. Through the porthole Delia saw Swarthyface and her father going ashore in a small dinghy. She watched them clamber up the steep, wooded slope and disappear in the direction of Carstairs. She prayed that her father would come to no harm.

She realized that Lebb was busying

himself with various tasks on board the motor cruiser, for she could hear him moving around. She tentatively tried the door, but it was locked. In sudden anger, she banged hard with her fists.

Lebb came down immediately, opened the cabin door,

'What the devil do you want?'

'Why are you keeping me locked down here?' demanded Delia.

'Because then I know where you are. Is that all you want?'

'No. I want to go on the deck. My head is aching with the aftermath of that drug.'

Lebb considered.

'The boss says you have to be kept on board. Okay, come on deck, but if you think you can try any funny tricks, forget them. I'll slug you sooner than let you escape.'

Delia came up on to the diminutive deck behind the cabin. A strong breeze was blowing, and as she stood the wind pressed her dress close to her alert body. Lebb eyed her thoughtfully, and Delia noticed the look. She moved away in sudden fear.

In the back of her mind was the possibility of escape. Perhaps she could dive overboard and swim to the shore. But what possible use would it be? Swarthyface still had her father, and there might not be another Kennedy to appeal to for help — there would never be another Kennedy, she thought. She remembered his smile, his twinkling eyes as he looked down from his commanding height.

She was looking at the water thoughtfully. Lebb said:

'Don't try to escape. Anyway you can't. I could get you before you decided to jump.'

It was true. The deck was merely a small cockpit, and Lebb could reach her in less than a second.

Then a moment later Delia noticed a small speck of a boat about a mile and a half away — so far as she could judge. If she was not mistaken the boat was approaching them.

It was an interesting discovery. So far Lebb, too busy eyeing the girl, had not noticed. Delia wondered about the approaching boat. Probably some local yachtsman pleasantly spending his time.

If she began to wave to the boat, Lebb would force her down to the cabin. In any case, it was all so useless. If her father could not escape from Swarthyface, she would stay by his side.

The minutes passed and Lebb had seen the oncoming boat. It was a motorboat, judging by the speed with which it was travelling. Perhaps only ten minutes had passed, yet the craft had covered a fair distance and was now plain in outline. Delia saw the bows and the foaming water, but she could not see anyone on board.

Lebb was staring hard, and if Delia had wanted to dive overboard this was her chance. Lebb's suspicious mind was compelling him to watch the oncoming boat.

It was slicing through the sea at a powerful speed, and the bows were pointing straight at the *Firefly*.

With every second that passed, Delia's heart beat faster. There was something odd in the way the approaching boat was hurtling towards them. The boat was not idling the day away. This was not some pleasure-seeking yachtsman. This could not be coincidence.

Lebb was coming to the same conclusion. With a curse, he drew his automatic from his pocket.

To Delia came an exhilarating realisation. It was purely feminine logic, but she felt sure Kennedy was on the approaching boat. Kennedy and Clive! They were not dead. She knew it!

And with every minute it became obvious that the *Firefly* was the target for the oncoming boat. The newcomer was less than three hundred yards away. The sea foamed away from her bows. The beat of her engine could be heard like an avenging song.

Still no one was visible on the deck of the newcomer, but Delia was almost crying with excitement and suspense. She knew Kennedy was near. She knew!

Then Lebb turned with a snarl.

'Get down into the cabin.'

She stood defiantly, but he seized her arm and struggled with her. Delia resisted fiercely, but even so Lebb was a muscular man and Delia found herself pushed down the two small steps towards the cabin. She stumbled and Lebb pushed again, and clanged the door, locking her inside.

When Lebb raced to the diminutive deck again he found the newcomer was very close. Perhaps less than a hundred yards separated them.

Then Lebb received a shock. Quite distinctly he saw the faces of two men who should be dead. Two faces on the big motorboat stared grimly over the intervening stretch of water. Lebb cursed, realising that in some way the two men had escaped being burned to death.

Kennedy and Clive were on the boat. And at the wheel stood Mr. George Whiteman, who had found the big boat for Kennedy and insisted upon accompanying him so that he could identify the *Firefly*. With him was his son. They had made inquiries whenever they had reached hailing distance of any craft, and by this means had got on the trail of the *Firefly*.

Lebb raised his automatic and sent off two shots. He had the satisfaction of seeing Kennedy and Clive duck out of sight. Then Lebb carefully trained his gun on various parts of the motorboat. He shot up the portholes, thinking he might easily hit something. Lebb had definite ability as a marksman. He shattered two portholes and peppered the motorboat just below the waterline to see if he could wreck the craft. Then he reloaded his gun.

The big motorboat had stopped, with engine cut off. For an appreciable time there was no activity to be seen. Lebb watched closely, crouching below the rail of the *Firefly*.

Then all at once a gun exploded on the big motorboat. Lebb, expert on firearms, knew it was a rifle and he cursed and bobbed out of sight behind the bulk of the engine cover. The bullet bit into the hulk of the *Firefly*.

Lebb chanced a swift glance. He caught sight of Kennedy holding the rifle and Lebb took a pot shot and dived promptly for cover. A split second later a bullet nicked the rail a foot away. Lebb found a crack in the *Firefly's* woodwork whereby he could see the oncoming boat without exposing himself. It seemed that she was drifting slowly nearer.

His attempt to hole the craft didn't seem to be much of a success.

Either the bullets had merely lodged in the tough wood, or the leakage was negligible and easily kept at bay with an automatic pump.

In a sudden fury Lebb released a full barrel of shots at the motorboat, aiming for the spot where he had last seen Kennedy with the rifle.

In return came a number of rounds with the rifle, and Lebb lay flat on the boards, cursing. He was afraid of the greater penetrating power of the rifle. He was, he realized, in a sticky position.

And while he lay a swimmer left the big motorboat and, progressing strongly underwater, came under the *Firefly*. The swimmer had a shock of red hair, but no one saw that. As for Lebb, he was cautiously raising himself. He planned to get hold of Delia and use her as a hostage. If the others fired they would have to risk hitting the girl. That strategy would enable Lebb to hold off his attackers while he thought out a plan.

There was danger if Swarthyface returned to the shore unsuspectingly. He might be shot at and killed.

Lebb rose to a crouch and made for the cabin door.

Even as he moved a hand gripped the rail of the *Firefly*, and a red head appeared. Cautiously Clive drew himself up.

He saw Lebb's back, and knew that this was his chance. The gangster was unsuspecting. Clive put all his energy into heaving himself from the sea and into the cockpit with one lithe swing.

As his feet thudded to the boards, Lebb whipped round with a startled glance. He raised his gun and fired.

Clive fell simultaneously with the speed of a dive bomber. There was a distinct thud as he crashed to the boards, but his hands were within inches of Lebb's feet. He had beaten the bullet. In truth the shot had scraped his shoulder.

He stretched forward with a lightning

move and gripped Lebb's ankles just as the gunman pressed the trigger again. Even as the gun exploded, Lebb was jerked backwards by a violent tug and he came crashing down.

Lebb, experienced at many a rough-house, tried to retain his grip on his gun, but his hand struck a locker with painful force and involuntarily he reacted. The gun flew from his grip and clattered to one corner of the boat cockpit.

Then Lebb prepared to fight for his life. He grappled with Clive.

And Clive, determined to beat his opponent, got in first with a punch that a prizefighter would have envied. But Clive was dealing with a desperate man, and with the cunning of his kind, Lebb proceeded to employ all the dirty tricks he knew.

He gouged and kicked and sought to fasten his hands round Clive's throat. Clive, accustomed more to clean fighting, was distinctly at a disadvantage.

While Clive attempted to beat off the other with straightforward blows to the face and body, Lebb kicked and aimed for the other's stomach.

Eventually he landed a blow that sent anguish through Clive's entire system. Lebb grinned as the other momentarily dropped his guard, and Lebb's hands flew for the other's throat.

It was an unlucky moment for Clive. Clive had won the toss in order to carry out the swimming exploit and he groaned at the thought of failure.

But neither of the two combatants had noticed that the big motorboat was creeping nearer, that in fact less than ten yards of water intervened. Then in as many seconds the ten yards was closed, and a huge figure, carrying a rifle, leaped into the tiny cockpit of the *Firefly*.

Kennedy Balfour went straight for his enemy. He did not dither about niceties The rifle butt was raised and brought down on Lebb's head.

Lebb went sliding down without a groan into a mile-deep darkness,

'Got the swine!' said Kennedy with satisfaction.

'He nearly got me,' said Clive ruefully.

'Nonsense, Clive. You did splendidly.

Where is Delia and her father?' Without waiting for an answer, Kennedy dashed towards the cabin turned the key, which was still in the lock.

And Delia dashed into his arms. She had heard the shooting and seen the motorboat close up.

And then Kennedy realised that Swarthyface was not on the *Firefly*. A word and Delia rapidly explained.

'I thought it a minor mystery why Swarthyface did not show his ugly mug on this boat when we came up,' declared Kennedy. 'So the game is not yet ended. We have to round up the chief thug.'

13

Face Your Partner!

Swarthyface and Dixon Thomas stepped through the gloom of the ancient tunnel leading from Carstairs to the sea. Garcia was behind Thomas, and held an electric torch. The white light splayed on the walls of the tunnel, showing glistening moisture and black, age-old rock. A murky, sinister labyrinth, which had seen many dark deeds and tragedies, was this passage. Dixon Thomas wondered if another tragedy was to be enacted here, for he planned to resist at the last moment. It was a sorry, vague sort of plan — but if he could obtain Swarthyface's gun — turn the tables — kill Garcia!

At intervals Swarthyface uttered his peculiar jokes.

'Ah, my Thomas, we are very near the end of this useless quarrelling. Soon we work together, eh? Soon we find the pretty picture about which we fight so much.' And Dixon Thomas would receive a jovial poke in the back with Swarthyface's gun!

'A horrible place is this tunnel,' declared Swarthyface. 'For me — I like the sun and the air, yes and money. Where is the cellar?'

'It is not far away,' muttered Dixon Thomas. 'Perhaps another five minutes so far as I can judge.'

Still his plans to beat Swarthyface were only vague, weak ideas. Another few hundred yards of rough steps and Dixon Thomas saw the sombre iron door in the light of the torch. The very sight of the sinister cell was enough to bring shudders. To think that Delia had been imprisoned in the foul hole!

There was nothing else but to enter. The door was not locked; it swung open upon receiving a hefty push. The creak was ominous; Dixon Thomas heard it as if it was a grim, gloomy omen.

Thomas walked inside the cell. He proceeded to the other end, stooped and looked for the plate in its canvas wrapping.

'It is not here!'

There came an angry grunt from Swarthyface.

And then to their ears, in a moment of silence, came the strange sound of shuffling footsteps. They heard the dull clatter of stones grinding and slipping as someone came along the tunnel.

'Be quiet!' hissed Swarthyface.

Even in the face of this new event, he did not allow Thomas the opportunity to slip away or steal behind him. Swarthyface kept the other man in front of his gun, and switched off his torch.

They waited in the darkness, beside the iron door, for the unknown person.

The step came nearer, and then they were abreast the iron door. Swarthyface switched on his torch and with one swift jerk stepped to face the stranger.

Blinking in the light was an old man clad in fisherman's clothes. He backed like a frightened animal, and like a frightened animal he was fascinated by the glaring light.

Swarthyface grasped the situation in a flash. There was no danger. His finger relaxed on the gun trigger.

'What do you want my friend?'

And Dixon Thomas stammered out the facts before he realised their implications.

'He is the old fisherman who rescued Delia from this cellar. He knows all these passages under Carstairs.'

Swarthyface backed so that he could threaten both men with his automatic.

'So he is acquainted with the passages! Fool! This is the man who has taken the plate!'

'Now old man, where is the plate you stole from this cellar? You have it. A metal plate — you understand — with many fine lines upon the surface. Where is it?'

There never was an answer to Swarthy-face's question, for the next moment a shot echoed in the confined space of the tunnel and the gun leaped from Swarthy-face's hand.

It was a magnificent shot from a spot fifty yards down the irregular-shaped passage, and Kennedy had been guided by Garcia's torch. The automatic had shown plainly in the pool of light, and Kennedy had aimed at Swarthyface's hand.

Swarthyface tried to fight but Kennedy was in a grim, vicious mood. He saw the man who had tried to shoot him and ordered a girl to be tortured. He flung two punches at him. Then all his weight went into a ramrod left jab.

Swarthyface took the blow and fell. His head struck the rocky wall of the tunnel with a sharp crack. He lay still, sprawling like an apparition.

When Kennedy turned him over and examined him, he saw he was dead. The man had broken his neck on striking the tunnel wall.

'He's dead,' said Kennedy, straightening up. 'He broke his neck when he fell.' He smiled grimly. 'I suppose you could call it an accident — though I can't say I'm sorry it happened.'

Differing emotions were mirrored in Thomas' face — predominantly relief. 'At last! I'm free of his threats! Delia and I can live our lives without looking over our shoulder. A new start — '

Kennedy shook his head.

'We're not out of the woods yet, sir. You're forgetting about Swarthyface's body. How are we going to explain it to the police?'

Thomas looked worried. 'Do we have to? Report it, I mean?'

Kennedy considered. 'Maybe I could get Lebb to put it alongside the man he killed at Carstairs — wherever that may be!' He shook his head. 'No — too risky. If the bodies were ever found together, the police would assume murder for *both* of them, and that could be awkward — '

'That's it!' cried Thomas excitedly.

'What is?' Kennedy frowned.

'You said it yourself — '*if* the bodies were ever found'. The answer is to make sure that Swarthyface's body is *never* found, and the best place for that is right here in this cellar!'

Kennedy did not look too convinced. 'I agree it's a good idea, but is it foolproof? If old Joe can find his way here, then so could others! Don't forget these old tunnels come out at his beach cave.'

'The answer to that is simple.' Thomas was smiling. 'We can dynamite the tunnel at both ends. This cellar would then be buried under impenetrable rock. No one would ever discover it. I've actually had such an idea at the back of my mind for some time, only I was thinking of burying the engraving plate, not a body.'

Kennedy considered for a long moment — then:

'I do believe that's the answer, sir! Let's do it.'

They dragged Swarthyface's body into the cellar and left it — another grim relic for the ancient tunnels. Truly the old place could hide many secrets.

Dixon Thomas told Kennedy about old Joe apparently finding the engraving. In turn Kennedy had to explain how they had escaped the death Swarthyface and Lebb had planned, and how they had turned the tables on Lebb.

They induced old Joe to show them to his cave in the mouth of the tunnel, and they retrieved the engraving. Dixon Thomas looked at the plate, which had caused so much trouble.

'I'll destroy this,' he vowed.

Later, on the motorboat, he battered the plate with a hammer until the fine lines were unrecognisable. Then he flung it into the sea.

Soon, after much deliberation, they turned Lebb loose. There was nothing else to do. They could not kill a man in cold blood. But with the death of his employer Lebb realised he would have to seek new fields. Nor did he pose any threat to Kennedy or the Thomases: they had too much on him, and the threat of informing the police about his activities was sufficient to ensure that he would never come near them again. And with the death of Swarthyface the organization for forging bad currency would disintegrate, for the various underlings had not the power to work together.

The *Firefly* was restored to the Whitemans, and later Clive drank their health in cider.

There was one final detail to be attended to, before they closed off the tunnels. Delia and her father took the destitute fisherman Old Joe to the social authorities, and he was taken into care.

Kennedy, whose idea it had been, considered that it was unlikely that he would ever talk to his carers of his experiences in the tunnel — and even if he did, no one would believe it was anything other than delusional fantasy . . .

Kennedy came to Delia one day.

'Look here, darling, I've known you a month already. When do we get married?'

In his arms she whispered; 'Now, if you like.'

'Well, damn it, I love you so much I can't wait. I'll ring Clive and tell him to get ready to be best man.'

She smiled.

'I've never wanted to wait. Why have we waited? Can you tell me Kennedy, dear?' He grinned down at her.

'Well,' he confided, 'we wanted to see your father smiling again.'

THE END